# GUARDIANS OF THE CAMBRIAN LODE

CW00857978

Reuben Stone has lived in the Upper Towy Valley of mid Wales, the setting for *Guardians of the Cambrian Lode*, since 1978. His family, originally from south Glamorgan, resided for a time in Wiltshire, where the author was born in 1970.

When he enrolled as a college student at Aberystwyth, Reuben developed a reputation as a restaurant pianist. It was an experience that he would later find useful in academic work on music plagiarism: when called for, he was able to provide live demonstrations of perceived similarities between different compositions.

Reuben holds a PhD in law from the University of Wales. His area of research, intellectual property rights in motion picture films, led him from the West Coast of Britain to the West Coast of the United States, where he was a visiting scholar at Stanford Law School and an intern with the Lucasfilm Company. On one occasion, he made a brief appearance in front of the cameras for an episode of the *Young Indiana Jones Chronicles*.

On his return to Wales, Reuben completed his doctoral thesis and then began writing a work of a very different character. You hold the result in your hands.

# GUARDIANS
*of the*
# CAMBRIAN LODE

**REUBEN STONE**

BETHANIA BOOKS

London

This edition published in Great Britain in 2005 by
Bethania Books, 145–157 St John Street,
London EC1V 4PY
Email – admin@bethaniabooks.co.uk

First published in Great Britain in 2005 by Bethania Books.

Text © Reuben Stone 2005

Reuben Stone asserts the moral right to be
identified as the author of this work in accordance with
the Copyright Designs and Patents Act 1988.

All rights reserved.
No part of this publication may be reproduced,
stored in a retrieval system, or transmitted, in any form
or by any means, electronic, mechanical, photocopying,
recording or otherwise, without the prior written
permission of the publisher.

Scripture quotations are taken from the New King James
Version®. Copyright © 1982 by Thomas Nelson Inc.
Used by permission. All rights reserved.

A catalogue record for this book is available
from the British Library.

ISBN 0 9550034 0 7

*Cover art by Mari Lois.*

Book design and production for the publisher by
Bookprint Creative Services,
P.O. Box 827, BN21 3YJ, England.
Printed in Great Britain.

For
Jacob, Tywi,
Medi, Teilo and Tesni.

# *Acknowledgements*

To all those who have inspired me, provided me with advice and given of their time to help prepare my manuscript for publication, I offer my sincere thanks. In particular, I am indebted to: James and Gwyneth Davies, the Revd Dr Eifion Evans, Patrick Hutchings, Lewis and Bethan Jones, and Dr Brinley Jones.

Finally, I wish to thank my parents; for without their encouragement and support, the story that follows would never have made the transition from imagination to the printed page.

RS

# Contents

*A tribute
to those who followed the Way
at the dawn of Christendom;
a rallying call
to their successors in the last days.*

# CHAPTER ONE

# The Wanderer From Afar

During the Roman Occupation of Cambria, there lived in the upper reaches of the Towy Valley a tribe known as the Ewenni. These folk, and others like them, were what remained of a scattered band of ancient Britons, driven into the far west by the advance of the Imperial frontier. There, in the wilderness, the Ewenni were left undisturbed – until events intervened in the year of our Lord 303.

It had reached that point in the seasons when the green excesses of summer growth give way to the purging hand of winter's first whisper – when creatures of the air yearn to journey south, the oaken leaves forewarn, and the bracken on the skyline turns.

On a certain afternoon in those days of long ago, an observer positioned at just the right point on the Towy River would have noticed a boy of the Ewenni tribe – Rhidian by name – standing near the water's edge. His purpose in being there, the observer would soon have discovered, had a great deal to do with the kind of contraption that has come to be known as a waterwheel; for there, situated at the edge of the river, was just such a device. Its supply of water came from a fast-flowing stream that cascaded into the Towy from a height of some twelve feet. Reaching almost to that level itself, the wheel was a striking piece of carpentry and would have seemed a picture of efficiency, but for one thing – it appeared to be motionless.

To Rhidian, it was a dispiriting spectacle; for the construction of the wheel had been his idea. If it couldn't be put back into operation soon, there would be trouble from certain members of the boy's own tribe. They had only been persuaded that the wheel might be of benefit to them on the basis that it could be used to perform mechanical tasks – in particular, the operation of a quern, or grinder, for crushing certain kinds of rock. In short, the waterwheel had been intended to act as a labour-saving device. Rhidian had even been reckless enough to describe it as such to his tribe. The way things were going, however, it wasn't too difficult to imagine how the boy's initial optimism might now be turned against him. Indeed, some were already referring to the waterwheel as *Rhidian's folly*, a grim epitaph indeed for a project that had once held such promise.

What, then, was the matter with Rhidian's wheel? In essence, the contraption had been suffering from the effects of a phenomenon that was most unusual for the Cambrian region – a lack of rain. Over the course of the previous week, Rhidian had done his best to make up for this unwelcome development. He had tried to ensure that the water from the stream was properly directed into the buckets around the rim of the wheel and that, once there, it could not escape from the system too quickly. In this way, as little energy as possible would be wasted.

At first, these innovations had proved effective and had enabled the waterwheel to continue rotating for a few days longer than it could otherwise have done; but now that the volume of flow in the stream had diminished yet further, the system had finally ground to a halt once more.

As he stood there, pre-occupied with his predicament, the boy was suddenly startled by a sound in the nearby undergrowth. Moments later, the figure of a man emerged above the river bank. His weather-beaten appearance and grey hair seemed to indicate that he was a person of some maturity, if not of considerable age; but his movements were remarkably agile nonetheless. He came quickly down the bank and was soon at Rhidian's side.

"Do not be alarmed," began the stranger, evidently aware of the unsettling effect his sudden appearance had caused. "I seek only an audience with the leader of the Ewenni folk."

"Then," replied Rhidian, "you must be looking for Brân, the chieftain of the tribe."

The stranger nodded. "He will prosper greatly if

he heeds my counsel this day."

"Counsel?" inquired Rhidian, dubiously. "I don't think Brân has ever been much of a one for *that* sort of thing. Besides, he rarely speaks to strangers."

"I am no stranger to Brân. Now be a good fellow and tell him that Aaron, the pedlar, wishes to see him."

Rhidian shook his head, slowly. "It would be a mistake – for me, that is. You see, my work on this waterwheel is far from over. If I were to return to camp now, Brân would be furious."

"Indeed," murmured Aaron. "Well then, maybe you could simply . . . show me how I might find Brân for myself."

As he spoke, the pedlar glanced at the waterwheel. He frowned, as if he had spotted something amiss, and began to examine the contraption carefully.

"It is as I thought," he murmured, finally. "Your wheel has yet to be modified."

"Yet to be modified!" exclaimed Rhidian. "Why, that's absurd. If you only knew the work I've put into those buckets . . ."

"Ah yes – the buckets. Now that's my point. May I speak frankly?"

"You seem to be doing that already."

The stranger sighed. "Don't misunderstand me, my friend. There is much about this wheel of yours that is excellent. It is just that it could be improved . . ."

To Rhidian's astonishment and alarm, Aaron suddenly drew a dagger from his belt and thrust it straight

14

into one of the wooden buckets in the rim of the wheel.

"Wait!" cried Rhidian. "You'll cause a leak. We need *more* water in the system, not less!"

"Indeed we do, and that is what we shall have – *if* you will allow me to continue . . ."

A little stung by what had amounted to a mild rebuff, Rhidian fell silent. He waited anxiously while Aaron took up his dagger once more and proceeded to cut holes in the bases of each of the buckets around the rim of the wheel. The pedlar then gave the contraption a push. At first, it seemed as if nothing would come of this; but then, slowly, the wheel began to turn of its own accord. Within a few moments, the system was working at a steady rate, a development that Rhidian naturally welcomed with great relief and enthusiasm.

"Well, young one," said Aaron, with evident satisfaction, "now will you introduce me to the elders of your tribe."

"That I will," replied Rhidian, gratefully. "But, first, I should like to know the purpose of the holes in the wheel. Why, the water doesn't even splash out of the buckets any more."

"The secret," said Aaron, "is to allow any air in the system to escape. Those holes of mine allow for that. When water enters a bucket with a hole, the air underneath can escape, enabling the water to enter the bucket more easily. In that way, the system can operate with less water than would otherwise be the case."

"By the way," added Aaron, peering into the stone

15

grinder beside the waterwheel, "what material is it that you are crushing here?"

"A mineral," replied Rhidian, simply.

Aaron extracted a piece of rock from the grinder.

"Ore of lead?" he inquired.

Rhidian nodded. "We've been smelting it for the past month now."

"Indeed," said Aaron, gravely. "Then there are now *two* reasons why I must meet the elders of your tribe. Pray lead me to them, boy."

Even without the assistance of Rhidian, the Ewenni encampment would not have been difficult for Aaron to spot; for some of the younger members of the tribe had already begun to light their fires for the evening. Nevertheless, with the boy to introduce him, Aaron's reception at the camp was made a good deal easier than it might otherwise have been. Before long, the pedlar was being ushered into a gathering of the tribe elders. Among these folk were Rhidian's father, Elgan, and his mother, Gwawr, but the chieftain of the tribe himself had yet to arrive; not that this fact seemed to be hindering anyone at all, for most of the Ewenni folk were busily engaged in the art of eating salmon.

"Rhidian?" said Gwawr, in a reproachful tone. "What are you doing here? Now, I told you earlier, it's no food for you until that waterwheel is up and running. A fine state we'll all be in if it still isn't working by tomorrow when our buyer comes. No food, mind you!"

"No indeed!" echoed Elgan, firmly.

"It's fixed," said Rhidian.

"What is?"

"Why, the waterwheel, of course."

"And the grinder?"

"That too."

Temporarily speechless, Gwawr snatched her husband's portion of salmon and handed it to Rhidian.

"Here, son," she whispered. "Take it all. Eat as much as you want."

"As . . .much as you want," muttered Elgan, between clenched teeth.

Such was the general appetite for helpings of fish that Aaron was left in peace for a while; but once the craving for food had passed, conversation soon followed.

"So," said Gwawr, finally, "we have a traveller in our midst. What brings him to these parts, I wonder."

Aaron shrugged. "A pedlar such as myself must replenish his supplies from time to time."

"Ah – then you must be headed for the Roman mines at Dolaucothi."

"I have no business with the Romans," replied Aaron, slowly. "Besides, it seems that their much trumpeted vein of gold at Dolaucothi has been mined almost to extinction. No, I shall not be venturing in that direction."

"If you do not trade in gold," noted Gwawr, "then there is only one other thing you could be dealing with in this area: lead."

"A lead merchant!" cried Elgan. "Why, then, the pedlar has come to the right place and no mistake!"

"The right place? I think not!" came a voice from somewhere outside the gathering.

Everyone turned to see who it was who had spoken. The person in question could plainly be observed emerging from the shadows. It was the chieftain of the tribe, Brân. He sat down next to the fire, his eyes malevolently fixed on Aaron.

"Our lead is not for sale, pedlar," continued Brân, coldly. "At least, not to *you*."

"It seems, then," replied Aaron, "that you already have buyers for the metal."

"Indeed we do. They pay us well."

"Not well enough, I'll warrant."

Brân's expression hardened. "What is it to you, old man?"

"I know what happens to those who work the ores of lead. Their fate is not a pleasant one. The fumes see to that . . ."

"That's as maybe, pedlar; but if it weren't for those fumes, we would have no yellow powder – and without the powder, we would lose our keenest new customer."

"New customer?" queried Aaron. "And who might that be?"

Brân shrugged. "A local fellow – goes by the name of Towser, I believe."

"Towser? Of the Gwenfo tribe?"

"You know him?"

18

"How could I not? All who know the Gwenfo tribe know Towser, reckless experimenter that he is."

"Reckless or not, he was here less than an hour ago. He took a whole sackload of powder away with him."

Aaron frowned. "If what you say is true, then there may yet be time to stop Towser from using the powder."

"Pah! Why would we wish to do that? The powder is of no concern to me."

"That is because you are ignorant of its properties – and of much else in these matters, it seems . . ."

Brân glowered. "I think the time has come for you to leave, pedlar."

"As you wish."

At that moment, a sudden noise, like that of a thunderclap, ripped through the air. It was followed by a series of echoes – eerie and long-drawn-out they were before, finally, they subsided, leaving the valley in a state of uneasy calm.

"So," muttered Aaron, "it has begun."

"Speak plainly, pedlar," replied Brân. "What is it that you fear?"

"Listen – do you not hear it? Something is happening – upstream."

"In the river, you mean? Nonsense! I hear nothing."

"Then will you believe the evidence of your own eyes? Behold: the waters are beginning to surge."

It was true. There, scarcely less than a hundred paces away could be seen the crest of a small wave, with some floating debris, advancing downstream at a considerable speed. So unsettling was the phenomenon that it caused all those gathered around the camp fire to withdraw to safer ground up the banks of the river.

That the debris had something to do with the mysterious sound that had been heard earlier seemed almost certain; but precisely what the explanation might be was unclear; at least, to Rhidian. Aaron, on the other hand, wore the kind of expression that suggested he knew rather more about these events than he had so far revealed, an impression that was quickly confirmed by what happened next.

Just as the last of the debris passed by, Aaron let out a sharp cry. He ran down the bank and waded into the river, far enough to arrest the progress of an object that was floating along in the water. After examining it carefully for several moments, the pedlar finally turned with a grim expression on his face.

"It is as I feared," he said. "Towser has perfected his powder – and paid for it – with his life."

"His life?" asked Elgan. "You mean, that's Towser's body you have there?"

Aaron nodded. "If I am to convey his remains back to the Gwenfo tribe at Blaencwm, then I shall require some assistance."

"I'll help," said Rhidian, at once.

"You'll do no such thing, boy!" growled Brân.

"But why?"

"The domain of the Gwenfo is no place for a boy of the Ewenni tribe. Have you forgotten all that we've told you about it? About the burial mound there? And the ghosts that lurk within?" Brân gestured towards a distinctive conical-shaped hill in the distance. "Behold, the *Barrow of Blaencwm.*"

Aaron laughed. "Nonsense, Brân. I know the hill at Blaencwm well enough. There is no barrow there; nor are there any ghosts. There is only the Gwenfo tribe and a very solid and down-to-earth folk they are too."

"Down-to-earth, you say? Hardly. They are like you, pedlar – worshippers of a strange god – a man who died over two hundred years ago."

At this comment, there was much laughter from the gathering on the river bank. Aaron seemed unmoved.

"The one of whom you speak," said the pedlar, finally, "did not remain dead for long. He is alive today. If you would but receive him, he would be not merely the god of the Gwenfo, but of the Ewenni too."

"I have heard you speak of this before," snapped Brân, "and my answer remains the same. We have no need of this god of yours. Do not waste your breath, old man."

"If that is your last word, then I shall take my leave of you. But, beware: what has happened here today is a warning to you all – a foreshadowing of what is to come. Therefore, I say, if you value your lives, you may have to abandon this encampment, and soon. An enemy may come upon you with no warning. If you leave here, head upstream until you reach the place where the waters meet at the Doethia. The Gwenfo tribe will observe you and help you when you reach that point."

"Be gone, pedlar," replied Brân. "We have no need of your counsel.

"And, if I were you," he added, coldly, "I should leave Towser's body to the river. You are too old to be hauling dead things through the wilds."

"Aaron won't need to carry the body," said Rhidian, slowly. "My mule will take it for him."

Brân looked as if he was about to explode with rage.

"If you do this, boy," he rasped, "you will be banished from the camp this very hour. How brave do you feel? Brave enough to face the wild beasts of the night on your own?"

His heart pounding with trepidation, and with the whole tribe staring at him in seeming disbelief, Rhidian left the gathering on the river bank and went to fetch his mule in one of the nearby fields. He then led the animal back down to the river and helped Aaron place Towser's body over it.

"You show commendable courage, young one," whispered the pedlar, "and it will be rewarded. At any rate, we shall see to it that you have nothing to fear from the wild beasts this night."

Secretly handing Rhidian a small green vial, Aaron continued: "I notice that you carry with you a bow. If you should ever be in danger from either man or beast, place a drop of the resin from this vial on the tip of one of your arrows. Even the slightest of wounds resulting from loosing such an arrow will quickly cause the victim to fall asleep, thereby enabling you to escape from danger. Have a care, however, that you do not touch the resin yourself, for its effects are indeed powerful!"

With that, Aaron gave a final wave and was off into the moonlit night. For a time, Rhidian watched his steady progress along the river bank; but soon the pedlar had disappeared from view, leaving those who remained to ponder the disturbing implications of all they had been told.

# CHAPTER TWO

# *The Prisoner at the Ford*

True to his threat, Brân's first act once Aaron had gone was to banish Rhidian from the Ewenni camp. The boy would have to fend for himself that night, hardly a cheerful prospect with such a long wait ahead until daybreak – a wait that would inevitably be accompanied by the distant, and not-so-distant, cries of lurking predators.

It was therefore with a sense of unease that Rhidian found himself pacing outside the perimeter of the Ewenni camp. He quickly decided to move to a place that seemed comparatively safe – next to some canoes moored along the river, from where he might be able to make a rapid escape, if necessary. Eventually, the boy lay down in the bottom of one of the canoes. The gentle, rocking motion had such a calming effect on Rhidian that it sent him gradually off to sleep.

It is doubtful whether the boy would have closed his eyes so readily had he realised what was about to happen; for, in fact, his canoe was not properly secured.

The extra weight it was now carrying was making it sink further into the water. Due to some overnight rain higher up the valley, the river had begun to swell and it was this effect that finally pulled the canoe free of its moorings and into the current. Within a few moments, Rhidian was being carried in his sleep much further than he had ever been in his life before while awake; past the crop plantation, the fishing grounds and the usual hunting areas. He might have ended up being washed straight down the river and out to sea if the canoe had not first become entangled in a fallen oak stretched across his path. It was the jolt of impact with this tree that finally awoke the boy.

Rhidian's first reaction on discovering his plight was one of fear and confusion. Where was he and how had his canoe reached the position it was in? Had someone in Rhidian's tribe untied the canoe from the river bank in order to be rid of him? These were some of the thoughts that filled his mind as he climbed out from beneath the branches of the old oak. This was not an easy task with the foaming current of the river constantly at his heels; but at last the boy's feet struck the warm, dry pebbles at the river's edge.

From his new position, Rhidian could soon see that the canoe had come to rest just above a wide and relatively shallow section of the Towy. It was clearly a crossing point or ford of some kind; muddy tracks led directly to the water's edge on either side of the river.

The canoe was still firmly wedged in the tree but,

as far as Rhidian was concerned, it could stay there. The boy had no intention of returning home on water. The quickest way back, in any case, would be to follow the river upstream on foot until the tribe camp came into view.

Rhidian was about to make a start on the journey home when he began to smell smoke. It seemed to be coming from a grove of trees just a short distance away. Perhaps someone was about to cook breakfast, thought the boy. His mouth watering with anticipation, Rhidian made his way in the direction of the smoke; but, unfortunately, the sight that greeted him was not quite as he had imagined it to be.

There, in a clearing and standing beside a camp fire, were three men dressed in helmets and armour. Although he had never seen them before, Rhidian realised at once that they must be Roman soldiers of some kind. His father had often warned him against coming into contact with such people. They were said to be suspicious of mountain folk and quite capable of killing any strangers whom they perceived as a threat. Rhidian had no intention of putting the matter to a test and would have sneaked away quietly at that point had he not felt so curious. What were these soldiers doing on their own in the wilds away from their comrades? It wasn't necessary to wait long to find out. They seemed to be talking to someone seated on the ground. As he crept closer to the clearing for a better view, Rhidian could see that this other person was a young girl of about his own age. Her hands were tied behind her back and she was staring at the three men with an expression of defiance and contempt.

The man whom Rhidian took to be the most senior of the three soldiers opened his mouth to speak but was interrupted.

"You have no right to detain me in this way, Sulla," yelled the girl. "I am a Roman."

"Indeed," replied the man called Sulla, with a sneering smile. "That is precisely what makes you, by your conduct, a traitor to your family and to the Emperor himself."

"A traitor?" echoed the girl. "I suppose that's what you would call someone who doesn't share the same ideas as you do about the Roman Empire. When my father hears about this . . ."

"Your father is in no position to object. He has yet to return from his expedition to the border marches. It is *we* who are in control here now. If your reasons for being in this area at such a critical time are entirely innocent, which I doubt, then we would be delighted to hear your explanation."

There was no response; the silence seemed to aggravate the man, for his face hardened and his voice changed in tone to a menacing growl. "Do you really think that your sympathies for the barbarian tribes and your lack of loyalty to Rome have gone unnoticed? Why else should we find, in your quarters, icons of our former enemy Caractacus and yet none of the Emperor himself? The truth is that without the protection of the Roman army, young lady, your life would be but cheap at the hands of these supposed friends of yours. We are all that stands between you and chaos in these islands."

The girl scowled. "If the army is as all-powerful as you say it is, how is it that you have failed today in your aim of capturing the Gwenfo tribe?"

"Your knowledge of military affairs is indeed impressive for one claiming to be so innocent," observed Sulla. "Unfortunately, the tribe in question has eluded us, alerted no doubt by some informant . . ."

"I had nothing to do with it," objected the girl, quickly.

"Spare us this pretence of innocence. Your story will soon change."

At this point, Sulla removed his sword from its sheath and placed it in the fire. He continued: "Of course, you are not the only person whom we believe to have knowledge of the Gwenfo. At this very moment, my men are questioning others who may have heard of them. So you see, young lady, there really is no point in further resistance. Save your remarkable courage for a more profitable occasion and tell us what we wish to know."

A ghastly silence fell upon those gathered around the fire as the sword slowly absorbed heat from the glowing embers. Meanwhile, Rhidian was becoming increasingly tense. It was too late for him to leave now with his conscience intact. He had become an unwilling participant in the drama being played out before him. He would have to do something to save this girl who, to judge from everything that had been said, was evidently a friend of the tribespeople; but what exactly should he do? Then the boy remembered the vial of poisonous resin that Aaron had given him for use in shooting with his bow. Hurriedly, he took the vial from its attachment on his belt and began to prepare the arrows.

"The time has come for us to have an answer, young lady," declared Sulla, grimly. He removed his sword from the burning brands and inspected it with relish, his nose twitching from the waves of intense heat emerging from its point. "You see, it is really quite cool. The blade isn't even white; it is just a soft red."

The sword was within singeing distance of the girl's neck now and yet she still gave no visible response despite the inner fear she must have been experiencing.

"We have run out of time. You had your chance to explain yourself in a civilized manner . . ."

Just at that moment, proceedings were interrupted by the sound of a horse approaching. As the creature came into view, it became clear that its rider was yet another Roman soldier. Sulla was clearly rattled by the distraction at such an important point.

"What is it?" he barked.

"There's still no sign of the Gwenfo," announced the messenger, nervously, "but we came across some other people close to the target area who are now being held by us."

"More again? Where are they now?"

"About five thousand paces upstream. We wondered if you might like to make an inspection and begin the interrogation."

Sulla sighed heavily. "In truth, I find the asking of questions a tiresome occupation but it is a necessary one if we are to expose the facts. I will accompany you, messenger."

Sulla mounted his horse and then threw a backward glance at his prisoner. "Do not think, young lady, that your ordeal is over yet. Regard it as merely postponed."

Then the man spurred his steed and, accompanied by the messenger, made off upstream along the river bank, leaving the remaining two soldiers to guard the girl.

The fast-changing circumstances had left Rhidian breathless. He was feeling particularly annoyed with himself for not being quick enough to loose an arrow at Sulla while he had had the chance. On the other hand, reasoned the boy, if he had actually shot Sulla, the messenger would still have arrived on the scene and might then have escaped to bring help; and that was without taking into account what the other two soldiers might have done. All in all, perhaps things were better as they were. Nevertheless, after having gone to all the trouble of smearing his arrowheads with poison, Rhidian felt it was time to show the Romans that were left in the clearing what he thought of them; so he carefully prepared his bow, drew back a shaft on the string and released his first arrow. It struck one of the soldiers on the upper arm. Clutching at the wound, he staggered for a moment before hitting the ground unconscious. The other soldier raced desperately for cover, correctly anticipating that he would be the next target; but it was too late. He also was hit by an arrow and, after experiencing the same symptoms as his comrade, toppled helplessly to the floor.

Rhidian emerged from his hiding place beyond the clearing, his hands trembling with shock. The girl seemed equally shaken by the pace of events although she recovered soon enough to give her rescuer a relieved smile and to introduce herself, by name, as Valeria. Once free of her bonds, with Rhidian's help, she went over to the bodies of the soldiers and examined them closely.

"They're not dead yet," she murmured, sounding disappointed.

"No," said Rhidian. "And they're not likely to die. The poison I used on the arrowheads will just make them sleep."

Valeria looked curious. "But you're a Celt aren't you? I mean, as a bloodthirsty barbarian, you must be cutting people's throats every day. They never told us anything about sleeping potions during our history lessons about the Celts."

"I suppose I'm not really a very good example of one," said Rhidian, feeling a little ashamed that he had not come up to the girl's expectations.

"Well, you look pretty authentic in other ways," she

remarked, eyeing the boy's rather wild appearance. "Anyway, we'd better do something with these bodies before they revive."

On Rhidian's suggestion, the two of them began dragging the limp forms of the two soldiers to the canoe which was still entangled among the oak branches in the river. The task of moving the bodies was an unpleasant one, made worse by the knowledge that their victims might wake up at an awkward moment; but, finally, the work had been done, with the bodies placed side by side in the bottom of the canoe.

"Let the river take them and decide their fate," murmured Valeria, giving the prow a push with her foot. Before leaving, the two of them watched the canoe being drawn into the current and round a bend in the river.

The camp fire in the clearing was still burning and Rhidian and Valeria fell down by the side of it, feeling exhausted by the events of that morning. Valeria found a box of food she remembered seeing earlier and the two of them set about eating the contents with a keen appetite. There were the remains of some dates, spiced loaves and fruit; but most exciting of all was the joint of venison that had been roasting away over the fire earlier that morning, just out of Valeria's reach.

Rhidian would have feasted away with more enthusiasm if he had not been feeling a little anxious about his people back home. The tribe would, no doubt, be concerned about his whereabouts. Or at least, thought the boy, his parents would be. Brân, the head of the tribe, would not have been too troubled, perhaps.

Valeria must have noticed the signs of concern on Rhidian's face, for she commented on the fact and asked him what was wrong. The boy then told his story from the moment when he had met the pedlar to the moment of his arrival in the clearing.

Valeria listened with much excitement and then laughed. "Fancy that! You went to all this trouble just to rescue me."

Then, like Rhidian before her, Valeria's brow furrowed over. "You know, I have a story too," she said. "Except that, unlike you, I left home deliberately."

"For the sake of the Gwenfo tribe?"

Valeria stared at Rhidian. "Of course! You overheard my conversation with Sulla. That's how you know about my connection with the Gwenfo folk. A proper little eavesdropper, aren't you? Yes, the Gwenfo have been very much on my mind. I have something to give them – a piece of parchment. Someone gave it to me in Alabum."

"*Alabum*? You mean, the Roman fort just south of here?"

Valeria nodded. "It was where I lived until yesterday; and where my father, the fort prefect, was living too until not so long ago. He had to leave on a mission to the east last week. That was when Sulla and his men came on the scene. They came to relieve the garrison while my father was away; at least, that was one of the

34

reasons. There was another: to do with the fact that Sulla is a decurio, an envoy of the Emperor Diocletian, appointed to inspect mining facilities in this region – like the gold mines at Dolaucothi."

"But there isn't much gold left at Dolaucothi, is there?"

Valeria smiled. "That doesn't stop people like the Emperor and Sulla from forcing us to send more slaves down the mines."

"Slaves?"

"Of course. How else could you retrieve the gold? In fact, I shouldn't wonder if that's what Sulla will do to the Gwenfo tribe if he finds them – turn them into slaves. That's after he's extracted some information from them – the location of the *Cambrian Lode*?

"*Cambrian Lode*? What's that?"

Valeria stared at Rhidian in seeming disbelief. "You're a Celt and you haven't heard of the *Cambrian Lode*? Save us! It's a vein of gold that is supposed to lie hidden somewhere in these hills, except that no-one seems to know where."

"Oh, I've heard of *that*," said Rhidian, quickly. "Only we don't call it the *Cambrian Lode*. In fact, we don't call it anything in particular. Most people seem to think it doesn't even exist."

"I tried telling Sulla that," muttered Valeria, "but he wouldn't believe me. I'm just glad he didn't find my piece of parchment. It could be something important. The man who gave it to me certainly thought it was. He turned up in my quarters, right out of the blue, when Sulla arrived. For some reason, the poor fellow seemed frightened. He begged me to take the parchment and get it to the Gwenfo folk as soon as possible. Then, just after he left me, he was arrested by Sulla. I saw it happen near the barracks. What took place after that is anyone's guess."

"Do you think the man you met is still alive?"

Valeria looked dubious. "The important thing now is to do what he asked and hand the parchment to the Gwenfo folk. I know my father would agree. There's no love lost between him and Sulla. After all, as Father would say, we owe *our* allegiance to Constantius Chlorus, Governor of these islands, and not, as Sulla does, to the Emperor of the East, Diocletian . . ."

Rhidian and Valeria might have continued their conversation and their meal for hours had they not been disturbed by a sudden noise.

"Hear that?" said Rhidian. "Sounds like horses on the march and people shouting."

Valeria groaned. "Not more arrivals, please! I thought Cambria was meant to be a quiet backwater of the Empire but this place is worse than being on the Appian Way at noon!"

Rhidian decided that the easiest way to spot the source of the noise was to climb the nearest tree and so, followed by Valeria, he used a conveniently placed oak for the purpose. It wasn't necessary to clamber up very far to see where the commotion originated. Fast

36

approaching them, and much too close for comfort, was what looked very much like an army of Roman soldiers, conspicuous in their red tunics and bright metallic armour. The chances were, they were Sulla's men.

CHAPTER THREE

# The Fate of the Ewenni

It seemed to the two in the tree that the safest thing for them to do at that point was to stay put. If they climbed down from their perch, they would be placing themselves directly in the path of the approaching army with very little time to make an escape. On the other hand, in staying put as they were, they would just have to hope that no-one would glance upwards into the leaves as they passed by underneath.

When Rhidian saw that it was Sulla who was leading the procession, the boy felt like kicking himself. If only he had insisted on leaving the clearing as soon as he had freed Valeria, the two of them would not have been in this mess; but then, how could they have known that Valeria's tormentor would return so quickly? He had only been gone for the space of less than half an hour and, according to what had been said by the messenger, he would have had a long journey ahead of him. For whatever reason, thought Rhidian nervously, Sulla had met up with his men earlier than anticipated.

As the line of people drew nearer, it became clear that a large number of them were not Roman soldiers at all. In fact, as might have been expected, the soldiers were leading a group of tribespeople. The only question was, who exactly were they? Had the Romans at last managed to capture the Gwenfo tribe and, if so, had these unfortunate individuals been interrogated concerning the possible location of the *Cambrian Lode*?

It was Rhidian who first realised the terrible truth. When the procession reached the clearing below, the boy had to stifle a scream. For he could see that the people whom the Romans had taken prisoner were not the Gwenfo; they were members of Rhidian's own tribe. Only the day before they had been feasting with great merriment beside the river. Yet now they were chained together and stumbling along miserably in single file, their heads heavy with shame. They were surrounded by soldiers; anyone attempting an escape from this march would have needed to outrun the pack of black dogs that menacingly shadowed the procession.

It was at that moment that the awful truth finally dawned on Rhidian. Aaron had clearly been right to warn the Ewenni of imminent danger; for the danger was all too apparent now.

Rhidian noticed Brân, the leader of the Ewenni, being marched along. He was doing his best to keep up with those in front but his only reward at that moment was to be given a sharp kick from one of the soldiers for straying too far out of line. He fell to the ground, only to be dragged to his feet again as the march continued its relentless progress. If only Brân had taken Aaron's advice by moving the encampment to safer grounds, the whole tribe would have been spared this catastrophe.

Then, to Rhidian's horror, his parents came into view. Their shoulders were hunched and they were already limping from the effects of forced marching but these were merely the outward signs of the suffering they were no doubt enduring.

Rhidian was beside himself with shock and anger. He felt he had to do something to stop his family being taken away, but as the boy started to climb down from the tree Valeria held him back.

"You can't help them now," she whispered, urgently. "If you try, those soldiers will just clap you in irons, like the others. We must find another way."

"But this may be our only chance," choked Rhidian.

Valeria squeezed his hand, reassuringly. "No-one knows the Roman mind better than me. Sulla would not have bothered to take any prisoners at all unless they were of use to him alive. Once we have discovered where they are to be held, we will be in a better position to plan a rescue; but not before." The girl's voice trailed off on noticing that the marching had stopped. Then someone began to speak to the assembled soldiers and prisoners. The voice was instantly recognisable; it belonged to Sulla.

"Here we take our leave of the river, across the Ford, and head for Dolaucothi, and the fort of Luentinum, through the Claerwen Pass. Any man, woman or child who cannot keep up with the rest is to be put to the sword; for those who are shy of marching will scarcely be fit to work in the Emperor's Mines."

Sulla then addressed his own men. "Legionaries of Rome. I ask you to bear witness to the absence here of two of your brethren in arms; the two men who were ordered to guard the prefect's traitorous daughter. There will be a reward for the man who finds these deserters and, more importantly, for the man who finds the girl. She may possess the knowledge we seek of the Gwenfo, and I am wary that such an enemy of Rome should be permitted to walk these parts freely. For the present, I shall assign ten men to the task of searching. The remainder are to journey on with me."

With that, the procession began to move on its weary way once again. There was a good deal of splashing as it crossed the river at the Ford but then, once across the other side, the noise of trampling feet gradually ebbed away into the distance.

Yet the watchers in the tree knew they were still not safe; for, although Sulla was now safely out of the way, ten of his men had been left behind. What was more, so had an uncomfortably large number of muscular black dogs from the prisoner pack. However, to the surprise of the onlookers in the tree, Sulla's men did not bother to conduct a search of the immediate area. It had evidently not occurred to them that the fugitives might either be so cunning, or so stupid, as to be dangling just

42

above the heads of their pursuers. Or, if the possibility had occurred to the men, it had perhaps been dismissed by them because, at that moment, their dogs were behaving in a normal fashion. As for Rhidian and Valeria, it was not altogether clear to them why the dogs had not reacted to their scents but they were thankful for it, nonetheless. Perhaps the many different smells lingering on the ground, from soldiers and members of Rhidian's tribe, had had the effect of confusing the animals. In any event, the clearing was soon empty of people, once more, and the two in the tree were able to drop to the ground and restore the circulation to their numbed limbs.

"Well," said Rhidian, in a dejected voice. "What do we do now?"

Valeria thought for a moment. "We'd better not go south of here. That would take us too close to the Roman fort at Alabum; besides, it would be more difficult to hide in the flat, open country down there. We can't go very far east at the moment without walking into the jaws of those dogs. Although it's tempting to try to help your people, I don't think it would be sensible just yet to move west in the footsteps of Sulla. We need assistance and I can think of no-one who can give us that other than the Gwenfo. After all, any enemy of Sulla's has to be a friend of ours. I say we try to find them and that means going north east of here."

Rhidian agreed: "We may even be able to meet up with Aaron. He said he'd be with the Gwenfo very soon.

43

If any one person can help us, he can."

It was Rhidian who spotted the horse first; but only Valeria could recognise it truly for what it was: an Arabian stallion of the kind prized by many a proud Roman centurion. Standing at a height of around fifteen hands, this pearl-grey creature, with its refined bearing and hoisted tail, would not have looked amiss on military parade through the streets of Rome; but it looked strangely out of place tied to a tree amid the lonely surroundings of the Cambrian wilderness.

Since Valeria had not seen the stallion earlier, it seemed reasonable to assume that Sulla's men must have left it where it was just before they had captured the girl. Whatever the explanation, Rhidian and Valeria were eager to take the opportunity presented by their find. However, although the stallion was fully equipped with reins, stirrups and saddle, it seemed reluctant to obey new masters.

Rhidian's efforts to befriend the horse proved fruitless. The animal kept moving off each time the boy placed his foot upon the stirrups; and when he finally did make it into the saddle, he quickly found himself being thrown back onto the ground. Fortunately, the beds of surrounding moss prevented any serious injuries and the boy was soon able to pick himself up with little more to show than a bruise or two; but it was what happened next that really bothered him. For as soon as she knew that Rhidian had recovered, Valeria herself approached the horse and its reaction this time

44

was very different from before. After spending a few moments talking quietly to the creature, and making sure that it had calmed down properly, the girl managed to swing herself into the saddle without so much as a flicker of resentment from the beast; it was as if it approved of the fact that it was now dealing with a Roman rather than a Celt.

Valeria wanted to call her new friend Trojan, after the wooden horse of a certain Greek legend, although Rhidian was not enthusiastic about either the name or the creature it was supposed to describe. In fact, Valeria at first had difficulty in persuading the boy to come anywhere near Trojan; but finally he agreed carefully to climb into the saddle behind Valeria, while being ever wary of the stallion's response. On this occasion, however, the stallion remained as unflinching as the real Trojan horse would have been.

Rather than risk losing their bearings by heading directly for the Gwenfo tribe over the mountain peaks, Rhidian and Valeria decided to set themselves on a lower course. They would proceed well above the valley floor but keep within sight of the river and its tributaries. In that way they hoped to avoid walking into any remaining pockets of Sulla's men, while being, for some of the time at least, just a short distance away from familiar landmarks. After all, in order to reach their destination, they would first have to pass through the home territory of Rhidian's people, the Ewenni. Rhidian felt sure that, once within that area, he would be able to find the Gwenfo tribe by following the directions that Aaron had given him.

At first, the route on which Trojan and his riders had embarked seemed straightforward enough. Patches of woodland on the valley slopes offered some cover to the passers-by underneath and, for a time, a network of animal tracks made for smooth progress. Even so, it was some time before the familiar features of Ewenni tribal territory came into view. As they drew nearer, Rhidian began to realise that nothing would be gained, and much would be risked, if he and Valeria were to approach the tribe camp; for the boy knew that no-one had escaped capture and that all of his people had passed beneath the tree in which he had been hiding back at the Ford. Besides, for the time being, the important thing was to reach the Gwenfo tribe at Blaencwm.

With that in mind, Rhidian told Valeria about a certain short cut, a trail that he and his family had sometimes used during the annual gathering of the sheep from the mountains. In the past, the trail had often provided a most effective means of outrunning escaping stray ewes. The boy felt sure that the way in question, if he and Valeria followed it across the mountain, would avoid the Ewenni camp altogether and lead to the slopes overlooking their objective.

When Rhidian spotted what he was looking for, Valeria followed his directions and turned Trojan onto the new trail. The sharpness of the ascent which followed tested the stallion's resolve to the limit. In fact, the riders were almost on the point of sliding off the horse's back when the gradient at last began to ease off and Trojan was able to heave his load the final few paces onto the mountain top. Yet even here, a certain sure-footedness was required in passing through the slippery combination of shale and heather that dominated the landscape. When their path eventually began to curve downwards, and the river valley came into view once more, Rhidian and Valeria decided that they would feel safer on foot for a while; so they dismounted and then took the opportunity to study their surroundings from the ridge onto which they had emerged.

Rhidian immediately noticed that they had strayed a fraction to the north of their intended target. This was clear from the fact that the *Barrow of Blaencwm*, as the Ewenni called it, was just to their left. It was a distinctive landmark by any standards although Rhidian had never been so close, nor had he ever come upon it from such an angle before. Had he lived in other lands, the boy might have taken it to be a volcano; for it was conical in shape, with a densely wooded base and a blunted, barren summit. Rhidian knew that he and Valeria would need to make their way to the far side of the Barrow; for that was where the Towy River flowed. Only on the far side, thought the boy, could there possibly be a "place where the waters meet", as Aaron had described it.

Rhidian and Valeria had become so involved in planning their next step, that they failed to notice the movements of Trojan. The stallion had begun to wander off down the mountainside. As soon as she realised what was happening, Valeria gave chase but, in doing so, she unintentionally spooked the horse into a canter.

The girl looked as if she was about to scream with rage; but she thought better of it and resorted to stamping her feet in the heather instead.

Rhidian watched the scene with a certain grim satisfaction; he had taken a dislike to the stallion ever since it had thrown him off.

"Perhaps you named your horse too soon," goaded the boy. "From what you told me of the Greek legend, I don't remember anything about the Trojan horse making a bolt for freedom. Anyway, I thought you had a way with horses."

"At least they don't throw me off in disgust," retorted Valeria, angrily. "I'm going to catch that horse, you may depend upon it."

"What's the point? We've already arrived at our destination."

"Don't you know how much an Arab stallion is worth?"

"No, but I do know what Aaron told me: to meet him at the place where the waters meet. Not to go chasing after horses; and that one, by the way, is heading much too far to the north of where we should be going."

Valeria began to run off down the mountainside, regardless. "You can try to find Aaron if you like, but I shall be looking for Trojan first. We may yet need a horse just to outgallop Sulla's men; and we can't be sure that your friend, Aaron, will turn up."

"Aaron will be where he said he would be. I would rather rely on him than on your horse."

Valeria was already some distance away and so Rhidian had to shout his final message. "Be careful, you reckless Roman! Watch out for the Gwenfo. If they're real Celts and they recognise you as a Roman, they may shower you with arrows first and ask questions later."

Valeria was moving on a course that would take her some way to the north of the Barrow; she had chosen her path for the time being and now it was Rhidian's turn to set about following his own. He struck a trail that would lead him south of the Barrow. This seemed likely to be by far the easiest way of reaching the river beyond.

The boy made a rapid descent into the valley below, helped by the sharp incline of the path he was following. With the Barrow now towering above him, Rhidian then proceeded through a patch of woodland round to the west of the landmark. As he did so, he began to hear the sprays of a weighty volume of water cascading along its bouldered course down the valley. The mists from the rapids were even beginning to betray their clammy presence upon Rhidian's brow. Yet it was perhaps with another presence, a very different one, that the boy should have been concerned: the presence that had discovered his trail and that was, even now, bearing down upon him, unseen. So pre-occupied had Rhidian become by the noise of the river ahead of him that he failed to hear the sound of a horse approaching from behind, failed to observe its rider dismount and failed to react even up to the last moment when a gloved hand reached out for his shoulder.

# CHAPTER FOUR

# The Pool of the Mingled Woad

Y ou would do well to be more on your guard, young one."

Rhidian spun round in shock, fearful of whom, or what, he might see; but there before him, to his great relief, was a familiar figure: it was Aaron.

"You are fortunate," said the pedlar, gravely, "that it was I who struck your trail and not one of the stalking beasts of the mountain wastelands; fortunate, too, that you were not being pursued by the men of Rome. Land of the wilderness folk this may be; but, of late, a traveller is as likely to come upon a legionary as one of the tribespeople; which, I fear, is how you must have come to be in possession of a creature of this fine pedigree." Aaron pointed at the horse from which he had just dismounted. It was none other than Trojan the stallion.

"But how did you know . . ."

"I observed your approach from the moment you appeared upon the ridge, yonder. When your horse galloped off down the mountainside and then wandered into these woods, he seemed eager enough to stay with me; but, be that as it may, we have more important matters to discuss. For the Romans are on the march again."

"Romans," echoed Rhidian, bitterly. "If only I had known more about their ways before today, it might have been possible for me to save my tribe."

"Even if such knowledge had been available to you, it would have made no difference. The fact is that, for many a year now, the Romans of the Cambrian Region have been on good terms with the tribespeople. I, for one, had no reason to suppose that had changed; until today, when my eyes witnessed the remains of the Ewenni camp."

"But it was you who warned us that we were about to be hit by a disaster. Surely you remember that?"

"Indeed I do; but it is one thing to receive a premonition and quite another to interpret the fullness of its meaning. That insight was denied me on this occasion. I can only think that it was in accordance with God's purpose for my understanding to be incomplete. It grieves me to have to say so, Rhidian, but I am convinced that, in this matter, the wrath of God has been visited upon your tribe just as surely as the Roman yoke."

Rhidian felt shaken. "But what has my tribe done to arouse the anger of your god?" he cried.

Aaron sighed. "A great deal, young one, a great deal; and it is my belief that your chieftain, Brân, must take much of the blame. Many are the abominations he has committed in the name of false gods, sacrificing innocent blood on the ancient stones in high places; and he has taught others to do the same. Did you not know these things?"

Rhidian shook his head.

"Brân cannot say he has not been warned," continued Aaron. "Yet always it is the same. He refuses to accept what I have to say: that if he continues in his ways and does not repent, he will be condemned to hell – to eternal separation from God. Indeed, such would be the fate not only of Brân but of all who refuse to accept the good news."

"Good news?"

"Concerning the Lord Jesus Christ . . ."

"You mean, the man you spoke about back at the camp – the one who died over two hundred years ago?"

"He died, yes – on a Roman cross; but then He rose from the dead, proving that He is what He claimed to be: the Son of God. Like a sacrificial lamb, He paid the penalty for our sins, so that by trusting in Him we may be forgiven and made righteous in God's sight."

"Do you think that even *Brân* could be forgiven his sins?" asked Rhidian.

Aaron nodded. "Even Brân."

"Is there anything that *cannot* be forgiven?"

"There is something. It is called the unpardonable sin and is perpetrated by those who commit blasphemy against the Holy Spirit."

Aaron must have noticed a look of concern on Rhidian's face, for he gave a reassuring smile.

"I do not think you have yet committed the unpardonable sin, young Rhidian; but, even so, you should take the opportunity, while there is still time, to accept the Lord as your Saviour."

"Perhaps," replied Rhidian, dubiously. "But first I must rescue my tribe. They need my help."

"What better way to help them than by becoming a follower of the Way – a follower of Christ – for then you would have the Lord on your side against the enemy."

"Against the enemy? You mean, Sulla?"

At the mention of the Decurio's name, Aaron winced. "If the person who took your tribe captive is who I think he is, then we are all in greater danger than I at first suspected. We shall need all the help that the Lord can give us. For this man whom you call Sulla is one of the chief persecutors of the followers of Christ. In truth, it would not be too much to say that he an agent of the devil himself."

"The devil?"

"Satan, the evil one, the devil; he has many names. It is he who opposes God's plan for mankind. The Lord will have complete victory over all the powers of evil; but that does not mean we can escape from the spiritual battle that is raging all around us. In this fight, we must put on the whole armour of God."

Aaron rose to his feet. "Come. There is something which you must see. It is time for us to strike the river and follow it to the place where the waters meet, also known as the *Pool of the Mingled Woad*. I am hopeful that when you have taken the time to ponder the mysteries of the waters, much that now remains beyond your understanding shall be made known to you."

With Trojan in tow, Rhidian followed the pedlar to the river rapids nearby. It took them all a little longer to reach the point further upstream that Aaron had in mind; but reach it they finally did. There, stretched out before them lay a body of water of a most remarkable character. Rhidian had no doubt that they had come upon the spot known as "the place where the waters meet". For what better description could there be of a pool situated, as this one was, where two rivers collided.

To this mingled mass of moisture from the mountains, there was something of a jade-like tinge. It was a phenomenon seemingly caused by sunlight being quenched among the waters and then dispersed through the natural hues of innumerable living organisms. Yet even more remarkable still were the unaccountable eddies and the surging pockets of energy of indeterminate origin, bouncing from the depths to break the surface at random.

"What *is* this pool?" murmured Rhidian.

"It is many things," came the reply. "To the passer-by, it is merely a pond of changeable mood where the Rivers Towy and Doethia become one. To the follower of the Way, it is endowed with the spiritual properties of a baptismal font and a fountain of rebirth; but to servants of the evil one, it is a site of conflict between opposing currents and undertows. For such men, I have seen these waters transformed into a bleeding cauldron. The question, Rhidian, is what does this pool mean to you? May I make a suggestion?"

"And what is that?" asked Rhidian, nervously.

"Dive into the midst of the waters, my friend."

"But I can't swim."

"Do you think that I would allow you to drown?"

"No, not really. It's just that – well – the pool is rather deep and the currents out there seem very strong."

"You are right. The pool is indeed deep and the currents are certainly strong; but were you not asking me, some moments ago, about the meaning of faith?"

Rhidian sat down firmly on the ground. "Aren't you asking rather a lot? I don't suppose Jesus would have expected anyone to step into water as rough as this."

Aaron gave a knowing smile, but said nothing.

"Look, I'm sorry Aaron," continued Rhidian, uncomfortably. "But I'm not ready. I really need more time to think about everything you've been telling me today."

"It is indeed good that you should think on these things; but think well, my friend, and do not delay for the sake of delay. For the paved byways of reason can bear us only so far before the fords of faith must be trod."

Rhidian gazed out across the surface of the pool and cautiously tested the waters with his feet. "What were you saying, a moment ago, about this pool and the servants of the evil one?"

"Ah yes. Beware the onset of snow in the mountains and the coming of frost upon the slopes. For the ice loosens the red deposits of iron ore, high upon the banks of the Doethia River; and when the thaw comes, and the mountain meltwaters flow, the ore granules are washed downstream here – to the place where the waters meet. Know, then, that when the waters flow red with the ores of iron, the Doethia River is on the rise and the time of peril draws near.

"Observe, Rhidian, the natural rotations of this pool. The currents spin round in one direction only, do they not? That effect is caused by the forces of the River Towy. Yet, when the inflow of the Doethia becomes the more powerful of the two rivers, there follows a reversal of the currents. I am no Archimedes, my friend. I know little of mathematics, nor of the science of fluids; but I do know that when the Doethia gains the upper hand over the Towy and the rivers run red, there appears, in the midst of the waters, a great vortex – a whirlpool. It draws into its considerable bosom all things that are within reach and bears them down to the depths, tossing them into the submerged caverns that lead down into the bowels of the earth – even, as it were, to the gates of hell itself."

At this point, Rhidian decided to speak up: "Surely, Aaron, if this whirlpool you mention is caused by the amount of water in the Doethia, then heaven and hell,

God and the evil one, have nothing to do with it, do they?"

Aaron raised an eyebrow. "Do you think that the natural elements are not God's to command? Does He not control the wind and the rain, the snow and the thaw, life and death? Can He not cause a whirlpool to consume the servants of the evil one, if He so chooses? I believe that He can."

Rhidian felt unsure of this but, all the same, he withdrew his feet from the water. As he did so, he noticed something positioned just behind him. It was a large, upright slab of rock with an image upon it. Indeed, the paint that had been used to produce the image was still wet. However, what caught Rhidian's attention was the *subject* of the painting. That it was meant to be a depiction of Jesus seemed clear from the fact that the hands and feet of the man in the picture bore wounds like those that might have resulted from a crucifixion. Though the quality of the painting was not especially sophisticated, there was a certain compassion about the eyes and a nobility in the countenance that held Rhidian transfixed.

The boy might have remained rooted to the spot for some time had it not been for a sudden and unexpected noise that broke through the silence of the wilderness. It took the form of a curious, high-pitched screech, emanating from somewhere high up on the Barrow of Blaencwm.

"A buzzard?" suggested Rhidian; for the bird of that

name was a familiar enough sight in Cambria.

"We shall see," said Aaron, cautiously. "Come. It would be as well to investigate the matter."

# CHAPTER FIVE

# Valeria Encounters the Gwenfo

While Rhidian had been heading for his meeting with Aaron, Valeria had failed in her attempt to recapture Trojan, the stallion; it had disappeared into a patch of woodland and by the time the girl reached the trees, the creature was nowhere to be seen. In fact, what had happened was that Trojan had doubled back under the canopy of the leaves and had then galloped round to the south of the Barrow on a course that led towards Aaron and Rhidian. This left Valeria still heading north of the Barrow under the mistaken impression that she would soon find her wayward steed, perhaps grazing somewhere.

After much bad-tempered trampling among the fallen twigs of the wood, Valeria was about to charge out into the open again when she heard something that made her draw back sharply: the not-so-distant murmur of voices. Fearing the presence of Roman soldiers, the girl ducked down low and listened carefully. On reflection, she felt sure the sound was coming from her left, just beyond a certain knoll. She crept up to the knoll and peered cautiously over the edge.

It was soon clear to Valeria that if she was in any danger at all, it was not of the Roman kind. For there, in the meadow before her, was a gathering of about a dozen individuals, dressed not in the armour of imperial soldiery, but in the rustic, homespun garments that characterised the folk of the wilderness. Among those on view were men and women of various ages. They were seated on the ground beside what appeared to be a freshly planted yew tree. Standing next to the tree was a woman dressed in a green shawl.

Valeria edged ever closer to the gathering, the girl's curiosity beginning to overcome her initial sense of fear. As she approached, she began to detect the strains of what the woman in green was saying to her audience:

"As the sun rises again over the Dinas, and the otters bathe once more amid the watery haunts of the Doethia, let us give thanks to our Good Shepherd for guarding us through the perils of the night. May we be empowered anew to continue our work as custodians of the manuscripts from beyond the seas. Enable us, we pray, to save these treasures from destruction; and may yet more be plucked from the flames. We look to the day when the hearts of the legionaries in every land will be turned to your Word – that at the name of Jesus, every knee should bow . . ."

So *that* was who these people were, thought Valeria. They were Christians – followers of the Way. It explained a great deal, including the fear on the face of the legionary who had asked Valeria to take the mysterious piece of parchment to the Gwenfo folk; for if the Gwenfo were Christians, they would have plenty of enemies.

Valeria's thoughts were soon interrupted by the sound of people singing. They were accompanied by musicians playing flutes and stringed instruments. Although familiar with the bold drums and trumpets sounded by legionaries on parade, Valeria had never before come across the kind of rustic tones she was now hearing. The sounds did not last for long, however. No sooner had the musicians put down their instruments than the woman in green began speaking again; but this time, her tone was more brisk than before.

"Would anyone like to do a little translation work for me?" she asked. "From Greek into Latin . . ."

It seemed, to judge from the number of those looking the other way, that no-one was about to volunteer.

"A pity," sighed the woman. "Can't seem to find any keen translators in these parts. Perhaps we ought to include that concern as an item on the prayer list."

By this time, Valeria had managed to mingle among the people of the gathering and, rather to the girl's surprise, they seemed extremely friendly. One of the men, who introduced himself as Cadog, struck up a lively conversation. When Valeria asked him if he could tell her the name of the woman in green, the man grinned.

"She has many names – not all of them to her

liking!" came the cheerful reply. "She is Eifiona, the Chief Scribe and Keeper of the Scrolls; but, since she is a hard task master, we have bestowed upon her other, less flattering titles. Naturally, we take good care never to mention these in front of her!"

Valeria thanked Cadog for his help and, feeling a little apprehensive, made her way to the front of the crowd where Eifiona was standing.

The woman looked at the new arrival with curiosity. "You're a little younger than most translators I've seen; but you'll do."

"Oh, I'm not really a translator, as such," said Valeria, quickly, hoping to change the subject. "In fact, I came here for a different reason."

"But you are able to read and write in Latin and Greek, are you not?" persisted Eifiona.

"Yes, but . . ."

"Then you're translator enough for our purposes. Come; there is much for you to see before we begin our work. What is your name, child?"

"Valeria," came the reply.

There was an awkward silence as all those standing nearby suddenly realised the significance of the girl's answer. Finally, Eifiona spoke again; but, this time, there was a distinct edge of caution in her voice. "If my recollections are correct, the name Valeria is of Roman pedigree. Are we to assume that your origin and loyalties lie with the people of Diocletian?"

Valeria thought for a moment before continuing,

aware that much depended on her response. "If you are asking me whether I am of Roman parentage and ancestry, the answer is yes; but as for my loyalties, the Emperor Diocletian excites nothing but contempt in me."

One of the men in the crowd, Gwion by name, sounded suspicious. "Very cleverly put, I'm sure; but how do we know the girl is telling the truth? The value of our work here depends on keeping Romans away from the manuscripts. How can we do that if the legionaries should get to know of our whereabouts from some . . . informer?"

Gwion's comments seemed to agitate many of the other members of the gathering. Eifiona had to try calming everyone down again before she was able to turn back to Valeria.

"I think what they're trying to decide," said the woman, earnestly, "is whether you should be our guest or our prisoner. I, for one, believe that the matter would be far clearer if you would tell us your story from the beginning."

Valeria was only too happy to oblige in this and, as she related the facts to them, the girl could feel the attitude of those surrounding her becoming more sympathetic. There were shouts of outrage as Valeria described the fate of Rhidian's tribe and yet more cries of disapproval when the girl warned of Sulla's plans to capture the Gwenfo.

The man named Gwion whistled with alarm. "Did I

not warn you, Eifiona, of the dangers of conducting our worship here, out in the open. We must retreat into the Dinas at once until the peril has passed."

Eifiona nodded gravely. "On this occasion, you may be right. There are times when the sacrifice of martyrs is called for, but that time is not now. I believe that our duty is to protect the sacred manuscripts from destruction and, insofar as we may, to assist Valeria."

Valeria then explained that her friend, Rhidian, had intended to meet the pedlar, Aaron, at the "place where the waters meet". The mention of Aaron's name seemed to cheer everyone up considerably.

"Let us hope," said Eifiona, "that the boy has indeed met Aaron at the place where the waters meet; for that is but a short distance from here and I would greatly value the pedlar's counsel in these matters before us. We ought not to disturb Aaron and the boy by the waters, however; for it is a place of spiritual contemplation. Instead, we shall put out a special call signal to summon them to the Dinas as soon as they are ready."

"Would it not also be sensible," observed the man named Cadog, "for one of our number, myself for instance, to scout out the territory between here and the place where Rhidian's tribe have been taken? In that way, we shall be better able to take stock of our circumstances and to plan our next step."

Eifiona agreed and Cadog then promptly ran off to find his horse which, he said, was grazing somewhere nearby.

"By the way, Valeria," said Gwion, with a puzzled look, "why would this Sulla fellow want to find us, the Gwenfo? I mean, it isn't as if we have any worldly wealth to offer him."

"He thinks you do," came the reply. "He says that the Gwenfo have knowledge of the existence of a certain hidden vein of gold."

Much to Valeria's embarrassment, Gwion began to laugh uncontrollably. "Why, there is more gold in my wooden leg than in the Dinas, or in this valley, for that matter! I don't know where that Sulla fellow gets his information from, but he is clearly gullible. If we were talking of fool's gold, maybe I could understand it . . ."

"Enough!" interrupted the Chief Scribe. "I am sure that Valeria would appreciate a more sober response from us than she is receiving."

Eifiona then gave the girl a reassuring wink. "Do not think that I have forgotten about the Latin and Greek. Being a Roman as you are, it would be surprising if you did not have a knowledge of those languages. I will put your services to good use, have no fear."

Eifiona beckoned everyone to follow her and then led them briskly along a trail leading away from the yew tree where they had earlier been worshipping. The trail soon entered a patch of woodland. On the far side, the walking party emerged onto an open meadow, sweeping gently down past a stretch of running water on the right. Further along, the blades of grass began to thin out and in their place were strewn great shards of rock.

It seemed clear that this debris must have fallen from above, for Valeria could see what she assumed was the Barrow of Blaencwm again beginning to dominate the horizon to her left. The girl had realised that what she thought of as the *Barrow*, the Gwenfo described as the *Dinas*. Both Eifiona and Gwion had referred to it in that way.

Just as the path began to steepen sharply, Eifiona stopped, followed by the other members of the group. They were now situated at the base of a sheer face of rock, the surface of which extended smoothly upwards, interrupted only by the occasional bushy outcrop and a few gnarled creepers here and there. It was to one such creeper, in particular, that Eifiona directed her attention. She gave it a sharp tug and then stood well clear of the rock face. Her reason for doing so became clear when, moments later, the lower section of a rope ladder whistled through the air and jolted to a rest just short of the ground.

"You want me to climb that thing?" asked Valeria, staring nervously at the cords of twisted vine.

"Oh, it's quite safe," said Eifiona, pressing one of her feet down on the first rung. "We've been up and down a thousand times."

Valeria wasn't sure whether these comments made her feel any happier, or less so, but it was at least some consolation for her to hear that only one person would be allowed on the ladder at a time. Taking her cue from Eifiona's rapid ascent, Valeria reluctantly followed, rung by rung, up the rock face. To have walked about fifty paces along the ground would not have presented the girl with any difficulty; but it was quite another matter to cover the same distance vertically, with hands smarting from grasping the ropes and while being ever mindful of the potentially disastrous consequences of a slip of the foot.

Valeria soon discovered that the ladder fed into a crevice just below the highest point on the rock face. Once she had crawled through the opening, the girl found herself inside a low, rounded cave.

"Welcome to the North Door of the Dinas," boomed a disembodied voice from the darkness beyond.

The sudden noise startled Valeria; but, as her eyes became accustomed to the new conditions, she was able to make out the shape of Eifiona, who seemed greatly amused by the reaction she had caused in her guest.

Valeria's ascent had left the girl breathless; she was certainly glad of the opportunity to lie still for a while, in the cool of the entrance cave, until the other climbers arrived.

As soon as everyone was accounted for, Eifiona lit a torch with some flint she was carrying and then led her followers down a passage into the heart of the Dinas. At times, progress was hindered by the lack of daylight, although Valeria was surprised at the number of places where the sun shone through from above. At one such place in particular, Eifiona stopped.

"This," said the Chief Scribe, proudly, "is the

Reading Gallery. It is where we study our scrolls."

Valeria saw at once why the area she was in had been chosen for the purpose Eifiona had mentioned; for the space was illuminated from one side by a vast window in the rock – high enough so as not to distract would-be readers with too spectacular a view, and yet not so high as to allow rainfall to interrupt any activities taking place below. Around the "Gallery" could be seen great oak benches and tables covered with quill pens, inks and paper weights.

"You mentioned scrolls, a moment ago. Where are they kept?" asked Valeria.

Eifiona's response was to lead Valeria away from the Reading Gallery and on down an adjoining passage to another point within the Dinas. The "Manuscript Vault", as the Gwenfo called it, was in fact a series of interlinked caves. Unlike the Reading Gallery, the Vault had no source of natural light; nevertheless, it was illuminated by powerful torches, of a special kind, each of which consisted of a bowl-like base containing a burning, oily substance. Bathed in the glow of these lights lay rows of boxes, many of which were engraved with foreign-sounding names like Alexandria, Tyre and Corinth. Some of the containers had been opened to reveal the contents within.

"You see this?" said Eifiona, picking up a crumbling piece of manuscript from one of the boxes. "It's part of an old papyrus scroll. The trouble is that papyrus doesn't last long enough. It soon disintegrates, especially in damp conditions; so do most of the other plant-based writing materials. One of our tasks here in the Dinas, therefore, is to transfer the words from some of the more important documents in our care onto materials of a kind that will endure well over time."

"Like this, for instance?" asked Valeria, showing the Chief Scribe the piece of parchment she had been carrying with her all the way from Alabum.

Eifiona stared at the document as if she was being presented with a rare jewel.

"Where did you find this?" she inquired.

"I didn't," replied Valeria. "In fact, *it* found me. Or, at least, I was given it by someone – someone who felt very strongly that the parchment should be brought here to the Dinas."

"Indeed? Then he was a Christian, perhaps."

Eifiona took the document in her hands and began to examine it carefully.

"Ah yes," she murmured, "this is parchment all right – vellum, too. We can't get much of it around here, more's the pity – have to make do with ewe skins instead . . ."

"What about the writing?" asked Valeria, impatiently.

"Well, one thing's for sure, it isn't Greek or Latin."

"Yes, yes, I know."

"It's Hebrew – from the Jewish Scriptures."

"Oh – so you won't be interested in it, then."

"Why do you say that? The Hebrew writings are as

much a part of our Scriptures as the letters of Paul the Apostle. It is all the Word of God."

"The Word of God?" inquired Valeria. "You mean, the writing on this piece of parchment is too?"

Eifiona nodded. "As a matter of fact, the words you see there were spoken by God to one of the prophets of old."

"Could you write it down in Latin for me?" said Valeria, with excitement. "I could show it to Rhidian. He'll think I did it."

"What's more," added the girl, smugly, "then he'll have to admit that I was right to part company with him and follow the horse . . ."

"The horse?"

"It's rather a long story."

Eifiona was silent for a moment. Then she began to smile, mischievously.

"I have an idea," she said. "Why don't you do the translation yourself?"

"Me? Do a translation?"

"Of course. I told you I was looking for a new scribe."

"What about the Hebrew? I don't know any of the words."

"You will – just take a look at the walls of this Vault."

Valeria glanced at her surroundings. As she did so, she noticed that the rocks round about were covered with writing. There were columns of strange-looking symbols chalked alongside familiar Latin words.

"We call this wall a *translectionary*," said Eifiona.

"To the left are the most common Hebrew words starting with the first letters of the Hebrew alphabet; to the right are the words starting with the later letters of the alphabet. As you can see, the Latin meanings appear in the columns alongside the Hebrew. So all you need do to translate your text is to match the Hebrew symbols on the wall with the words on the parchment and then write down the Latin meaning one word at a time. Simple enough, isn't it?"

Valeria gulped. It had not escaped the girl's attention that if she was to attempt the task Eifiona had given her, there would be rather a large number of strange, new Hebrew words to contend with.

"Oh, I almost forgot," said Eifiona, with a tone of mock innocence. "You should bear in mind that, unlike Latin and Greek, Hebrew sentences start on the right and finish on the left. What's more, it can sometimes be difficult to work out where one word ends and another begins!

"Well, perhaps I'd better leave you and let you get on with your translation – assuming you still want to show it to Rhidian, that is . . ."

CHAPTER SIX

# The Council at the Dinas

While Valeria was attempting to decipher the meaning of ancient text, Rhidian remained baffled by a problem of an altogether different kind: how to explain the uncanny bird-like screech that had disturbed his contemplations by the pool.

After an extensive search of the undergrowth nearby, Rhidian and Aaron emerged next to one of the rock faces on the western side of the Barrow. Of the elusive bird, if indeed that was what it was, there was still no sign. Rhidian peered up into the trees, hoping to be able to spot possible sources of the earlier noise; but he could detect nothing out of the ordinary there. What *did* seem out of the ordinary to the boy, however, was that when he turned round to speak to Aaron, the pedlar was nowhere to be seen. Rhidian quickly scanned his surroundings in all directions; it appeared impossible for Aaron to have moved out of sight as rapidly as he seemed to have done.

The boy was about to begin shouting for his friend

when a hand emerged from the side of the rock face where Rhidian had been standing. The hand made a beckoning gesture and was accompanied by a muffled-sounding voice; it was Aaron's. Rhidian soon discovered the explanation for the confusion. Aaron had passed through a concealed opening in the rock face and was waiting beyond in what appeared to be a cave. At least, this was Rhidian's first impression of the place. Once inside, however, it became clear that this was no ordinary cave. Indeed, it might better have been described as a vertical shaft within the rock face, for any sign of a roof was lost above the shadows and lofty echoes of the interior.

Aaron suddenly began to point excitedly up at some object above him. Whether the pedlar had his eyes better trained to the darkness than Rhidian was not clear; but the boy saw the object only just in time to jump out of its way. It was a large basket, of a sort, and it was descending fast beneath the ropes to which it was attached. Moments later, the basket struck the ground, sending shale flying in all directions. Rhidian had the feeling that Aaron had seen these things before, for the pedlar did not seem in the least surprised by the arrival of the basket. Indeed, he hopped straight into it and invited Rhidian to do the same.

"Where are we going?" asked the boy, climbing into the basket with some reluctance.

Aaron tugged impatiently at the ropes, as if to signal to someone. "Why, we are on our way to meet the

Gwenfo, of course. They have summoned us to their presence. Of that I am convinced; for there is a green flag flying high upon the rock face outside. That buzzard call, the one we heard a moment ago, is the Gwenfo way of attracting the attention of friends without arousing the suspicion of enemies."

Aaron's explanation was interrupted when the ropes above him began to strain and the basket juddered back into motion again. This time, however, the contraption was being pulled upwards by the application of some mysterious, hidden force. However, the ride could hardly have been described as smooth. Indeed, for much of the time, the basket seemed to be dangling motionless rather than climbing. On occasion, Rhidian noticed that sunlight was penetrating the rock face from the outside, projecting its beams onto the black inner walls of the shaft. The rate at which these images crept past in the darkness provided the only reliable indication of the progress of ascent; at least, until the silence of the surrounding space gradually became overcome by something else – the rasp of a winding device of some kind.

Fearing that the basket might be drawn into what-ever mechanism lay above, Rhidian made ready to leap for the first safe piece of rock he could find; but he needn't have troubled, for the basket came to rest at just the right point – next to a ledge protruding from a passageway in the rock. Rhidian reached over to the shaft wall and pulled the basket safely onto the ledge.

77

As he did so, he noticed a man standing within the passageway, grasping what was presumably the other end of the basket rope. When the man saw that the basket had been safely raised, he slumped down, exhausted. Unsure of how best to introduce himself, Rhidian sidled over and put his hand on the shoulder of the figure crumpled on the floor.

"I'll be alright in a moment," gasped the man. "Didn't realise . . . there were two of you in the basket together. By the way . . . I've sent a messenger to let the rest of the Gwenfo know you're here."

By this time, Aaron was out of the basket and was standing beside Rhidian. At first, the pedlar seemed as taken aback by the scene as his companion; but, then, a flicker of recognition crossed his face. "Why, if my eyes do not deceive me, we are in the company of Iago, the lamplighter! But what manner of reception is this? On the occasion of my last visit here, Iago, was it not said that a great feat of engineering would be attempted within these walls? That a lifting mechanism would be constructed so as to operate without the intervention of the human hand? Yet, it seems to me that without the intervention of that human hand, the lifting mechanism you have revealed to us today could not function."

The man named Iago wearily shrugged his shoulders. "You are right, as usual, Aaron. Unfortunately, things will not be the same for us now that Towser is gone. No longer will we be able to harness the forces of nature to do our bidding, as before. That, Aaron, is why the basket in which you were travelling, a moment ago, can be lifted only by human strength and not by the alternative means that Towser had intended."

"What is this alternative means that you mention?"

Still breathing heavily from his earlier exertions, Iago pulled himself up from the floor and showed his guests a certain recess in the passageway. Mounted securely inside was a rather large cylindrically-shaped object. Rhidian recognised it immediately as a waterwheel, for the boy was only too familiar with such devices. A water chute led from an opening in the roof to a position just above the wheel; beneath the contraption, a convenient hole in the rock seemed intended to act as a drain. Yet the system might as well have been designed to run on sand, for there was no water to be seen.

Rhidian guessed that there must be some kind of holding tank higher up above the waterwheel; without such a thing, it seemed unlikely that there would be a regular enough supply of rainwater available within a receptacle as small as the *Dinas*. When Rhidian asked Iago about this, the man seemed surprised; he had not really expected anyone to be aware of what a waterwheel was, still less the details of its operation. Waterwheels, after all, were still something of a novelty in the Cambrian Region.

"The tank you refer to," said Iago, "is about seventy paces above our heads."

"Seventy!" declared Rhidian. "Why, the pressure of

79

water coming from that height must be tremendous."

"It is indeed. But, for some reason, it is still not enough to raise that basket off the ground."

"Didn't Towser test the system properly?"

"He said that the installation was complete except for one thing – but he didn't say what that thing was. Even when the water flows at full pelt, there isn't enough power coming from the wheel to lift a reasonable load. The result, as you saw, is that we have to pull the rope in by hand."

Rhidian walked over to the waterwheel and examined it carefully. For a moment, he couldn't quite work out what was wrong. Everything seemed as it should be: the chute at the top of the system was correctly positioned and the buckets seemed to be of the right size. They had even been perforated for improved efficiency in exactly the same way that the buckets on Rhidian's waterwheel had been perforated by Aaron the day before.

However, as he studied Towser's device further, it suddenly occurred to Rhidian what the problem was: the buckets were not pivoted at the correct angle. Since Towser had attached them in such a way that they were fully adjustable, the boy decided to remedy the defect. He angled the buckets further upwards so that any water entering the system would be trapped for longer. As a result of these modifications, Rhidian anticipated that the power of the wheel, when set in motion, should now be correspondingly greater. The question was: would it be great enough to raise a person up the basket chute?

His adjustments complete, Rhidian climbed into the basket and asked Iago to lower it all the way down to the bottom of the shaft.

"What has to be done to set that waterwheel in motion?" asked the boy, as the basket sank downwards.

"When you reach the bottom," shouted Iago, "look for the lever hidden behind the fern fronds and give it a hefty pull – that should open the tank and release its contents onto the waterwheel up here. I still don't think it will be enough to raise that basket, though!"

When he reached the bottom, Rhidian found the lever mentioned by Iago. It was conveniently located next to the spot where the basket had come to rest. In order to test the strength of the lifting gear properly, Rhidian loaded a number of heavy stones into the basket with him. Then he pulled the lever. The fact that the basket took some time to begin its ascent did not surprise the boy, for he had reckoned on there being a delay between the opening of the tank and the turning of the waterwheel; but what did concern him was the slow rate of the climb once it had begun. Indeed, it took so long for Rhidian to reach the top of the shaft that he fully expected to find not the waterwheel, but Iago pulling at the end of the rope again. Yet, to Rhidian's surprise, it was Iago who was the first to greet him from the ledge at the top of the shaft; and this time, the lamplighter did not look in the least out of breath.

"It worked!" cried Iago. "You have no idea what a

difference this will make. We won't have to carry heavy weights up rope ladders any more."

Rhidian wasn't so sure. He had a feeling that the system needed a little further adjustment for greater speed; but at least what had been done so far was an improvement on before.

"How would you like to become the next Master of the Elements here at the Dinas?"

Rhidian stepped out of the basket and onto the ledge. "*Master of the Elements*? What's that?"

"It was what we used to call Towser before he left us – on account of his extraordinary ability to harness to our advantage the four elements of earth, fire, wind and, most important of all, water. Now that Towser is gone, we are in need of a replacement for him. He always said he wanted to leave us with a worthy apprentice or successor. I can think of no better person to offer that position to than yourself. In fact, I must show you Towser's old notebook – the one he used to record all his experiments in."

"Oh. I don't think a notebook would be of much help to me – I can't read."

"Neither could Towser – not properly, anyway. His book is full of drawings, mainly. He left it with us because he was afraid that, without it, we might 're-invent the wheel'. At least, I think those were the words he used."

Iago ran a short distance down the passageway and then returned with what he said was Towser's notebook. Its pages were beginning to yellow with age and, to judge from its contents, it had probably borne witness to years of experiments by the old Master of the Elements himself.

Rhidian turned the pages of the volume with great excitement. It was clear that Towser had found answers to many of the same questions of the natural world that had perplexed Rhidian at one time or another; questions concerning the use of fire and the extraction of useful substances from minerals, for instance.

Before Rhidian had a chance to study the notebook further, the sound of someone approaching down the passageway brought the boy back to reality. Moments later, a woman dressed in green swept into view. This was to be Rhidian's first encounter with Eifiona.

For her part, the friendly Chief Scribe lost no time in introducing Rhidian to the Dinas. "I am sorry I took so long to reach you. Iago's messenger had some difficulty in finding me – I was showing your friend, Valeria, around our little home here. By the way, you are invited to an audience with the Gwenfo in the High Hollow."

The *High Hollow*, as Rhidian soon discovered, was another example of the Gwenfo pre-occupation with taming their natural surroundings to greatest advantage. Chosen by the tribe from among the many hidden places within the Dinas, the place essentially consisted of two parts. There was a vast main cavern, the walls of which were infused with distinctive traces of quartz and other minerals. Beyond this point lay a raised ante-chamber, of a sort, approachable from the cavern below by means of a series of roughly hewn steps. The ante-chamber was adorned with vivid banners and tapestries depicting certain historical events that, no doubt, had a special significance in the traditions of the Gwenfo tribe. Beneath these hanging decorations stood a wooden table of considerable length.

When Rhidian and his companions arrived upon this scene, they found the table already surrounded by members of the Gwenfo tribe. Extra chairs were soon brought along and Rhidian found himself being seated next to Aaron at the top of the table. Eifiona had a hurried conversation with the pedlar before taking a seat herself. Valeria was the last to arrive. She sat down at the far end of the table, where there were still a few spaces left, and that was the moment when her eyes met Rhidian's.

The boy had a feeling there was something in Valeria's expression that he had not seen before – a certain sheepish quality, perhaps. Rhidian had little dif-ficulty in guessing what the cause might be. It no doubt had to do with his earlier argument with Valeria con-cerning Trojan, the stallion. After all, the girl had insisted on rushing off to catch the horse when it had bolted and had not wanted to meet with Aaron first, a circumstance that had led to her being separated from Rhidian; and, as the boy was well aware, by his choos-ing to go on alone to meet the pedlar, the irony was that it had been Rhidian, and not Valeria, who had succeeded in retrieving the wayward stallion. The boy would have liked to have cleared the air with Valeria over what had occurred earlier; but before there was a chance to do so, Eifiona loudly seized the moment to begin discussions of a different kind.

"By now," began the Chief Scribe, "many of you will already be aware of the nature and purpose of this meeting. Earlier this morning, Roman forces, under the command of a man named Sulla, entered the Upper Towy Valley. They were responsible for an unprovoked attack, some three miles from here, on the territory of the Ewenni tribe. The tribespeople have been taken to the Dolaucothi Gold Mines and are all being held captive there; all, that is, except young Rhidian here, who was fortunate enough to be away from his camp at the time of the attack. We have reason to believe that, not content with his assault against the Ewenni, Sulla also aims to find us: the Gwenfo. Those are the facts; but what do they mean and what, if anything, can be done to assist Rhidian's tribe?"

The man named Gwion cleared his throat. "It is too late for us to do anything today. By the time we reached Dolaucothi, the night would be upon us. However, I see no reason why we should not plan something for tomorrow. How much do we know about this fellow, Sulla?"

"Having been questioned by him," observed Valeria, "I know full well what his true intentions are. His real aim is to find the *Cambrian Lode* – the rich vein of gold that is reputed to lie hidden somewhere in this region.

Sulla believes that if he can find the Gwenfo tribe, then he has found the gold. I gather, from what Gwion told me earlier, that there is no such precious metal in this valley. If we can convince Sulla of that, then I believe he would depart the Cambrian Region forthwith."

"If only that were true," said Aaron, pensively, "then much sorrow could be avoided. Unfortunately, Sulla's quest for gold, if it exists, is a mere appendage to his other activities in the service of the evil one.

"It is my belief that what we are witnessing in this valley is a symptom of the great struggle of our time between the persecutors of the faith and those who are sympathetic to our cause. Emperor Diocletian is no longer the master of events. I hear much talk on my travels of disagreement and dissension among those of high rank. It is said that Constantius Chlorus, Caesar of this corner of the Empire, has certain family connections with the Britannic Isles. Some of his friends are believed to be followers of the Way. I feel certain that he would be appalled to learn of Sulla's presence in these parts."

"Do you have any knowledge of the present whereabouts of Constantius?" asked Eifiona. "Perhaps we should send him a message."

"There are rumours that Constantius is now at Isca Silurum, the fort on the border marches; but that is nearly four score miles from here. Even assuming that our man was there, we would be hard pressed to send a messenger and receive a response within seven days. By then, it might be too late."

"But should we not at least make an attempt to get through to Constantius?" persisted Eifiona. "After all, we cannot be sure exactly *when* Sulla may attack us."

"Very well," replied the pedlar.

"Good," continued Eifiona. "You see, I know a person with just the right qualifications to write our communication – a person who probably knows Roman court protocol inside out . . ."

Valeria turned rather red, for she no doubt realised that the Chief Scribe could only be referring to her.

For Rhidian, the discovery that his friend's Roman connections were to be put to use came as little surprise. However, it was the question of *who* Valeria should be asked to write to that troubled the boy and he decided to make a point of saying so.

"What about your father, Valeria?" asked Rhidian. "Couldn't we send word to *him* and ask for his assistance?"

The withering look that quickly settled on Valeria's face told its own tale.

"My father," grated the girl, "could be anywhere between Deva in the North and Isca Silurum in the South. It makes no sense to write a message to someone whose address is unknown!"

"Oh," replied Rhidian, feeling distinctly rebuffed. It seemed clear to the boy that Valeria was still harbouring some resentment towards him over the earlier incident involving Trojan, the stallion. Forgiveness was evidently something that would not be won lightly.

"Well," said Iago, breaking what had become a rather awkward silence, "it seems to me that we must somehow mount an expedition to Dolaucothi and fight Sulla, if we have to . . ."

"I don't like it," responded someone at the far end of the table. "If this fellow really is looking for us, then it would surely be foolishness itself to introduce ourselves. That would be like walking into a trap."

"Nonsense. If we deal with Sulla before he attacks us, then the element of surprise will work in our favour. Not so the other way round. We must head for Dolaucothi in the morning and rescue Rhidian's tribe . . ."

Valeria interrupted: "You forget that the Ewenni are being held at the Dolaucothi Gold Mines. To mount an attack, and to attempt a rescue, against that site would be no easy matter, for it is heavily guarded and protected by the nearby fort – Luentinum."

"There is also the difficulty," observed Gwion, "of how to reach the Mines safely in the first place. From our location here, there are three main possibilities. We could choose to approach from the south, by following the path of the Claerwen River; from the east, by heading directly across the mountain wastes of Mallaen; or from the north, by journeying through the Vale of the Llyfnant and into that of the Cothi. Each of these ways have their drawbacks.

"The Claerwen route would pose particular dangers for us, since the main Roman trail from Alabum to Luentinum crosses that territory; and, as Rhidian and

Valeria know only too well, the Claerwen Pass was used by Sulla to march his prisoners off into captivity.

"The way across the mountain wastes may be free of Roman legionaries, but not without good reason; for it is a wilderness that harbours many unspeakable perils.

"The Vale of the Llyfnant Route does offer a certain advantage to us, as tribespeople. For it leads towards Dolaucothi through a certain narrow pass, known in the Celtic tongue as *Beddau*."

At the mention of this name, Valeria frowned. "I was always told to avoid wandering through that Pass. They say that many of the boulders on the valley sides there are dangerous and liable to fall on passers-by."

"That is not entirely true," said Gwion. "The boulders are usually safe enough unless pushed from above. When that happens, the stones rolling downhill tend to dislodge others in their path so that a landslide may be set in motion. It was just such a landslide, two hundred and fifty years ago, that crushed an entire cohort of legionaries at Beddau. To this day, in Roman ranks, the mere mention of the name of that Pass may cause the boldest of centurions to flinch. Indeed, it is my belief that, since the disaster, no Roman has ever dared to cross into the Vale of the Llyfnant through Beddau; which is why we Celts may journey there with a confidence that is denied us elsewhere.

Valeria looked doubtful. "I have heard that some Romans travel close to the Pass, on the Dolaucothi side, to visit a certain temple there."

"Ah, yes," replied Gwion. "It is a temple to the so-called god Mithras, built by Romans years ago to oppose what they believed were the evil spirits that had caused the great landslide at the Pass."

Aaron gave a hollow laugh. "If that was their intention, then they would have done better to have left the wilderness to fashion its own monument to the dead. For those who worship Mithras are in danger of communing with the very source of evil itself – the devil. I have witnessed Mithras rituals for myself and, believe me, they are a profanity, a grotesque distortion of our sacraments, and a denial of all we hold dear. A Mithras Temple, my friends, is a place to be avoided at all costs."

"But is there any evidence that this Temple is still in use?" asked Eifiona, impatiently.

"Not much," said Gwion, "although, oddly enough, the Romans have always kept a herd of white cattle in the meadows of Dolaucothi; it is said that the white bull, in particular, is of vital significance in Mithras ceremonies."

Eifiona had begun to drum her fingers on the table with irritation. "Perhaps we could discuss the mysteries of Mithraism on a more suitable occasion. It seems to me that we have not yet reached a conclusion on the most important aspect of our discussion: how to attack Dolaucothi itself."

"I was coming to that," protested Gwion. "Before becoming a follower of the Way, I put some thought into the question of how a small band of men might raid and plunder the mines. It would be difficult, because anyone approaching the site, from most directions, is liable to be seen from the nearby fort on the banks of the Cothi. Also, the mines themselves are well guarded whenever there is work being done there."

Valeria nodded. "Particularly the underground compound where the slaves are held. What's more, the entrance is barred by heavy iron gates. How do you propose to open them?"

"Well," muttered Gwion, "that's the problem. Does anyone have any ideas?"

Eifiona rolled her eyes with exasperation.

"I think I have the answer," said Rhidian, suddenly. "It's in this book."

The boy picked up Towser's notebook from where it had been placed on the Council table and waved it in the air. He had been leafing through it and studying the illustrations ever since it had been handed to him at the West Door of the Dinas. He opened the book and pointed to a series of diagrams on the last page. They showed what appeared to be a method for making a certain powdery substance.

"Cambrian powder," said Iago. "Towser's last great experiment."

"An experiment," added Aaron, disapprovingly, "that cost him his life. Remember the incident on the river? Once lit, the powder destroys anything that lies within its vicinity."

"Exactly," said Rhidian. "That's why we need it – to

91

blow those gates off the slave compound."

Aaron frowned. "Be careful, Rhidian; you are vulnerable. The devil will be trying to distract you from coming to know the Lord. Do not make it easier for the evil one by allowing yourself to be drawn into needless danger. Beware of traps. If you choose to make Cambrian powder, you will do it against my advice."

"Well," declared Eifiona, "no powder for us, then. That settles it."

"No it doesn't," retorted Rhidian, angrily. "If we'd had some of that substance back at the Ewenni camp, my tribe might never have been taken! The Romans won't have such an easy ride next time – not if I have anything to do with it, they won't. I say we need powder to enter the mines at Dolaucothi and powder to protect the Dinas against an attack. What does everyone else think?"

"I agree with the boy," declared Gwion, forcefully.

"Me too," added Iago.

The show of hands that followed demonstrated that, by a small margin, Rhidian's view was the prevailing one.

"Very well," said the Chief Scribe, reluctantly. "Commandeer whatever is required and proceed with your plan, Rhidian. Iago will show you Towser's forge – the cave where the Cambrian powder was made. In the meantime, perhaps Valeria would furnish us with a letter to be carried to Constantius, asking for his assistance. As for the rest of us, let us ensure that our supplies and weapons, such as they are, remain in order. I am hopeful that Cadog, our scout, will return soon to provide us with news of Sulla's movements. In any event, at first light in the morning, it will be necessary for us to divide our company in two. Some of us will form the raiding party bound for Dolaucothi; the remainder will take charge of the Dinas, to guard it against a possible attack."

CHAPTER SEVEN

# *Cambrian Powder*

Whe the council gathering began to disperse, Rhidian spotted Valeria leaving the High Hollow. Curious as to why his friend had departed so quickly, the boy decided to follow along behind. Valeria marched off down a narrow passageway and, at the end of it, disappeared through a door in the rock.

When Rhidian reached the door, and saw what lay beyond it, he stood open-mouthed; for there, before him, lay a cavern filled with scrolls – boxes of them. Never before had he come across such a vast collection of documents. Indeed, rarely before had he seen any documents at all!

Yet there, seated in among the boxes, was the familiar figure of Valeria. She did not appear to be in the best of moods. No doubt, thought the boy, Valeria had not forgotten about the earlier squabble between herself and Rhidian concerning Trojan, the stallion.

"Well?" demanded the girl. "What is it? Can't you see

I'm busy with these manuscripts?"

Rhidian felt a little taken aback. "Don't you need any help?"

"Not really."

"Look," continued the boy, awkwardly, "I know you're angry about what happened on the mountain and I'm sorry . . ."

"Sorry! I should think so! If we'd stayed together up there, we might have stood a chance of catching that confounded stallion."

Rhidian wasn't sure whether to feel angered or amused by Valeria's worsening temper; but he bided his time. "If it's Trojan you're bothered about, then don't worry. I know where he is."

"Oh you do, do you?" said Valeria, still annoyed. "I thought the original plan was that you were supposed to find Aaron, not Trojan."

"Since they both happened to be in the same place, it would have been impossible to find one without the other – trust me."

"I'm not sure that I *do* trust you, you Celtic barbarian! No doubt, the only reason you're offering to help me with my translation work is because you're hoping that, in return, I'll be persuaded to help you prepare that Cambrian powder."

"The thought had crossed my mind," admitted the boy, grinning broadly.

"Then the answer is no."

Rhidian shrugged. "Iago has offered his help; so it

wouldn't matter in the least if I didn't have yours."

Angrier than ever, Valeria reached over to the table in front of her, grabbed a small ink-pot and then threw it at Rhidian. It struck him squarely on the forehead, causing him to let out a yelp of pain.

When she saw the effect of what had happened, Valeria's mood changed immediately to one of anxiety. She rushed across to where Rhidian was standing and tried to comfort him.

"You are alright aren't you, Rhid? I really didn't mean to hurt you, of course . . . say something."

Now the truth was that although Rhidian was undoubtedly smarting from the blow he had received, he really did not feel greatly inconvenienced by it; but he was not about to let Valeria have too much satisfaction from the fact!

Valeria sat the boy down and then fetched a piece of cloth, together with a jug of water, from a corner of the Manuscript Vault. She soaked the cloth in the water and began to bathe Rhidian's forehead, rinsing away the traces of ink deposited there from the bottle that had been thrown.

"A little higher, please," suggested Rhidian, doing his best to sound shaken.

Valeria obliged, her fingers gently probing Rhidian's scalp for further signs of injury.

"And the other side? I think the bottle must have hit me there too."

"That's odd. You don't have any marks just there."

Rhidian closed his eyes and waited for the soothing motion of Valeria's cloth to begin once more; but, instead of this, the boy felt something very different – the unmistakable sensation of warm, soft lips upon his cheeks. A little startled by this turn of events, Rhidian's eyes popped wide open. Peeping back at him was a rather sheepish-looking Valeria.

"Listen," stuttered the girl, "I never really intended to say what I said earlier – you know, about Trojan and all that. It was mean of me. I don't suppose that offer you made earlier still holds, does it? You were going to help me with my translation work."

Before Rhidian had a chance to respond, Iago, the lamplighter, appeared at the entrance of the Vault. He seemed a little short of breath.

"Why, I've been looking for you everywhere. Hadn't we better start making that Cambrian powder before darkness sets in?"

Rhidian hesitated. He felt torn between his desire to stay with Valeria and what he felt was his duty to accompany the lamplighter. However, the boy knew that Iago was right about the question of darkness setting in. Once prepared, the Cambrian powder would need to be kept away from fire; this would prove difficult if it became necessary to produce the substance at night in the light of flaming torches.

Leaving Valeria to continue her work, Rhidian reluctantly followed Iago out of the Manuscript Vault, promising to return as soon as he could.

Towser's Forge, as Eifiona had described it, was located deep down in the bowels of the Dinas, well away from the most well-trodden areas. The purpose of this positioning, Iago cheerfully pointed out, was that should some mishap occur in an experiment, at least the only victims would be the unfortunate experimenters! As for the content of the Forge, this was the most remarkable aspect of all. Crowded into every available space could be seen many different kinds of apparatus, made of clay, metal or wood. There were crucibles, urns, sieves, pipes and pestles, all bearing the traces of past use. Located in one corner were three large barrels – the first containing a black powder; the second, a white powder; and the third, a yellow powder.

"Well," breathed Iago, "at least we won't have to go to the trouble of preparing each of the powders individually. Towser must have made this batch very recently."

"He didn't make the yellow powder," murmured Rhidian. "That came from the Ewenni."

"Your own tribe?"

Rhidian nodded. "My folk are skilled in the art of producing ingots of lead. Yellow powder can be recovered from the fumes that are given off during the smelting of the metal ore. As for white powder, though, I've no idea how *that* is produced."

"Prepared from bat droppings, by the looks of things," said Iago, staring at the illustrations in Towser's notebook. "And by a rather intricate tech-

99

nique, too. I'm glad we don't have to copy it! At least the black powder seems familiar enough."

Rhidian nodded. "Charcoal. Well, I suppose we'd better start mixing. Only, be careful. If the three powders combined are as dangerous as I think they are, we can't afford to take any chances!"

According to Towser's notes, the ingredients of Cambrian powder were to be mixed in the proportion of one part black and one part yellow to eight parts white. To achieve these proportions, in such a way as to ensure the substances were properly mixed, took some considerable time; and then there was the matter of transferring what resulted into containers of a suitable size. The amount of the substance, Rhidian felt, seemed a little disappointing in view of the effort that had been required to produce it. All in all, only five small wooden barrels were filled. Even so, the young Master of the Elements declared himself reasonably satisfied with the afternoon's work. It only remained to transfer the powder to the bottom of the basket chute, ready for use at a moment's notice the next day. The barrels were distinctive in appearance, each of them bearing a red top, an appropriate indication as to the perilous nature of the substance they contained.

As Rhidian and Iago made their way back up to the main caves of the Dinas, Rhidian explained that he wished to visit the Manuscript Vault to find out how Valeria had been progressing with her work. Replying that he too had some matters of his own to attend to,

Iago waved Rhidian off and left the boy to go his own separate way.

When he reached the Manuscript Vault, Rhidian found Valeria seated next to the trestle table she had chosen to sit by earlier. She was gnawing thoughtfully at the end of her quill pen and seemed not to have noticed Rhidian's arrival. It was only when the boy picked up a document on the table that Valeria raised her head.

"Do be careful with that, won't you Rhid? It's still wet. We don't want to present Eifiona with a letter full of smudges."

"What letter?"

"It's our request for help from Constantius – you know, the one everyone talked about in the council. We'll be sending it off in the morning. Oh, by the way, I thought you might just like to have this."

Valeria drew out a strip of parchment from beneath the table and handed it to Rhidian. It bore a sample of what appeared to be Valeria's handwriting.

"It's in Latin," added the girl, rather unhelpfully.

"I'm sure you're right," muttered Rhidian, throwing his friend a sideways glance, "but what do the words actually mean?"

*"The LORD does not see as man sees; for man looks at the outward appearance, but the LORD looks at the heart."*

"You're beginning to sound like Aaron. I thought you told me you weren't a follower of the Way."

"I'm not, but the passage isn't mine anyway. I translated it from that strip of parchment I was carrying all the way from Alabum. Eifiona tells me it's from the Hebrew writings – part of what the Gwenfo call the Holy Scriptures."

Intrigued, Rhidian turned the parchment over in his hands. It was quite a thought. He was holding what amounted to a portion of the sacred Scriptures, a part of the writings which, according to Aaron, the Romans had tried to destroy.

As these ideas were passing through Rhidian's mind, Eifiona appeared at the door of the Vault. After thanking both Rhidian and Valeria most warmly for their efforts that day, the Chief Scribe suggested that it might be sensible for everyone to turn in for the night, in view of all that was in store for the following day. Although they did not feel especially tired, Rhidian and Valeria felt that the advice was sound and so the two of them followed Eifiona out of the Vault, taking care to extinguish the oil lamps as they went.

That night, it was decided that everyone would sleep in the High Hollow, where the council had been held. The fire, from earlier in the day, was still glowing and some extra logs were thrown on to ward off the nighttime chill. Eifiona arranged for some beds of straw to be laid out in a circular pattern on the floor, a most welcome sight for the tired occupants of the Dinas.

It was agreed that, under the circumstances, someone would need to remain on guard while the others slept. Rhidian and Valeria offered to take the first watch, but Eifiona wouldn't hear of it. She insisted on them taking their turn, if at all, only after they had had plenty of sleep. They would be woken later, if necessary.

Aaron, Gwion, Iago, Eifiona and the others all drew straws to decide on the order of the guard; it was Eifiona who took the short straw for the first watch. She decided to start by positioning herself on the rocky overlook, near the basket chute, where the best views of the all-important southern approaches to the Dinas were to be found. Since the cloud cover seemed to have cleared, and there was a full moon that night, it was just possible that any approaching dangers might be spotted well in advance.

One by one, those left in the High Hollow took to their beds and dropped off to sleep, all except Rhidian and Valeria who continued to talk on in hushed tones for a while longer. Eventually, even they became weary and slept.

In the middle of the night, Rhidian suddenly awoke. He felt cold, for the fire in the grate had now burned down to just a few glowing embers. Worse still, Rhidian's muscles had started to ache from the effects of riding Trojan, the stallion, the day before. The boy tried to go back to sleep, but to no avail. Then Gwion appeared. It seemed that he had just completed his watch at the overlook. He tiptoed over to the place

103

where Iago lay and gave him a shake – presumably, thought Rhidian, because the lamplighter must be the next on duty. However, Iago seemed not to have reacted to Gwion's presence at all. Gwion was about to begin prodding the sleeping figure more aggressively when Rhidian stopped him and offered to take the next watch in Iago's place. Not unnaturally, Gwion seemed pleased to be relieved of his responsibilities. He made himself comfortable on one of the straw beds and, within a few moments, Rhidian was once again the only person left awake within the cave.

Taking a torch with him, the boy arose and followed the long, tortuous passage leading to the basket chute and the rocky overlook. As he emerged into the night air above Blaencwm, Rhidian could see the entire expanse of the river valley spread out below him in the moonlight. Yet apart from the distant cries of the usual creatures of the night, little else seemed to be stirring.

After he had been standing on the overlook for a while, Rhidian started to pace up and down in an attempt to relieve the aching sensation in his muscles. He was beginning to think that his watch would be as uneventful as Gwion's had presumably been when a sudden noise startled him. It seemed to be coming from below. Rhidian peered intently down into the valley beneath him. Sure enough, there, silhouetted against the banks of the river, something was moving. It was the figure of a horse, its rider slumped forwards in the saddle. Whoever the rider was, it seemed likely that he was injured and might be in need of some help.

Rhidian now found himself in a quandary. The boy was, of course, in a position to assist immediately, by using the basket chute; but that would not necessarily be the safest thing to do, especially if the person concerned was a Roman, or if there were Romans nearby. Besides, it would first be best to let someone else in the Dinas know what was happening.

On the other hand, if Rhidian had to go all the way back up to the High Hollow, where the others were sleeping, then a good deal of time would be lost and the person down below might be placed in increasing peril, either from his own injuries or from some other hidden danger of the night.

Then, suddenly, the sound of a buzzard call from down below persuaded Rhidian that it might be worth taking the risk of an immediate descent; for to give a buzzard call, as Aaron had once explained, was the Gwenfo way of attracting attention. The man down below was therefore, in all probability, a friend of the Gwenfo tribe. That, at least, was comforting to know.

Rhidian headed for the chute and used the basket to lower himself to the ground. Once clear of the entrance to the Dinas, the boy immediately spotted the horse. It was in fact a pony. Its rider seemed to have fallen off, for he was lying on the ground with one of his feet still resting on a stirrup. When Rhidian drew close enough, the fallen rider clutched at the boy's hand.

"I think it's broken," wheezed the man, pointing at

his leg. "Can you take it out of the stirrup?"

Rhidian carefully did as he was asked, pulling the rider clear of his pony and resting his back against a nearby tree trunk. The man was evidently in some pain. He stared at Rhidian with nervous curiosity.

"You have the appearance of a tribesboy; and yet I do not recognise you as one of the Gwenfo. You must be Rhidian, of the Ewenni tribe."

The man evidently anticipated what Rhidian's first question would be, for he continued: "Your friend, Valeria, related your story to me earlier. I am Cadog, the one whom Eifiona assigned to determine the whereabouts of Sulla and his men."

"And did you find them?" asked Rhidian, apprehensively.

Cadog pointed grimly at his right forearm and untied a makeshift bandage that had been wrapped around it. Underneath was a gaping wound.

"One of Sulla's men did that," he breathed. "I happened upon him by accident just beyond the pass at Beddau. That was when I fell off my pony and injured my leg. Fortunately, there was just enough time for me to haul myself back into the saddle and ride away. The enemy gave chase, of course, but I managed to give them the slip in the woods near the pass."

"That's miles from the Gold Mine," observed Rhidian. "What were Sulla's men doing *there*?"

"No doubt, you have heard of what lies on the far side of the pass: the Cothi Dam. At one time, the

Romans were very proud of this construction. It served the Mines at Dolaucothi with vital supplies of water for extracting and purifying the gold ore. Yet the Dam has now fallen into a state of disrepair, its channels silted up with mud and debris. That, you may be sure, is the reason why Sulla has visited the site today; for, without a steady flow of water, the Mines at Dolaucothi cannot be worked."

"Then, at least," said Rhidian, "Sulla has not yet been able to put my tribe to work as slaves."

Cadog looked grim. "I deeply regret to have to say it, Rhidian, but the people of your tribe were the very ones who were given the task of unclogging the Dam; and, what is more, now that their work there is complete, they will be taken back to the Mines in the morning."

"Then we must go to them at once!" cried the boy. "Our chances of rescuing them would be so much better at the Dam rather than at the Mines."

"Not so fast, Rhidian. There is a problem: your tribe are being held in the catacombs of the Mithras Temple at Beddau. The Temple itself is easy enough to enter, but the catacombs are not. A great iron door blocks the entrance and the strength of many men would be required to move it. You will need the help of the Gwenfo tribe to accomplish this mission, Rhidian. I only wish I could accompany you myself."

"You have played your part already, Cadog, and I am grateful to you. We must find someone in the Dinas to see to your leg."

"Ah yes. I shall ask Eifiona. She would have made a most capable medicine woman had she not decided to become a scribe."

"By the way, Rhidian, your friend, Valeria, told us that the stallion, Trojan, is not to your liking. You would be most welcome to take Eira, my pony here, when you need to ride next. She is of Cambrian Mountain stock and well used to bearing Celtic folk like us. You should have no trouble from her. I fear that I shall not be riding her again for some time."

After thanking Cadog for his offer, Rhidian helped the man up, half-carried him into the entrance cave of the Dinas, and sat him down in the basket at the bottom of the chute. Since he had not been present when the lifting mechanism had been fixed in place, Cadog seemed astonished to be told that he could now be transported straight to the top by the power of water alone. Not even old Towser, he observed, had quite managed to accomplish that.

It was therefore of considerable embarrassment to Rhidian when he found himself unable to set the basket in motion; the lifting mechanism seemed not to be responding to the pulling of the lever among the ferns. Thinking that perhaps the load was too great, Rhidian helped Cadog out of the basket and back onto the ground again; but still the system refused to start.

While Rhidian tried to think of ways of coaxing the lifting mechanism back to life, Cadog grew steadily more tired.

"Wake me up," he yawned, "when we reach the top."

Yet Rhidian had soon exhausted all his ideas. He became convinced that only someone at the top of the chute would be able to set the waterwheel in motion, if at all.

The boy was already regretting the fact that he had not told someone else within the Dinas about Cadog's arrival; for the Gwenfo tribe would still be fast asleep, unaware of the events occurring less than a hundred feet below them. There was little point in shouting, for the sounds were unlikely to pierce the solid rocks of the Dinas. The only folk who might be drawn to such a commotion were prowling Roman legionaries. No, the only thing that could be done, thought Rhidian, miserably, was to wait in the hope that someone in the Dinas would wake up of their own accord; but, by that time, Sulla and his slaves would probably have left the Dam at Beddau and they would then have to be pursued to Dolaucothi itself, a hazardous undertaking indeed.

When Rhidian turned to ask Cadog for advice, he found that the man had fallen asleep. Under the circumstances, there seemed little point in waking him.

It was at that moment when Rhidian noticed, out of the corner of his eye, the barrels of Cambrian powder that he had placed in the cave earlier. In a flash, an idea occurred to the boy. Was it possible, he wondered, if the explosion of a casket of powder could shift the iron door described by Cadog – the door which was said to block the entrance to the catacombs where the Ewenni were being held? If it was possible for the powder to be used successfully in this way, then what was to stop Rhidian mounting a rescue attempt on his own? It was true that Cadog had an injury to be seen to, but there was little Rhidian could do for the man. Besides, he seemed as comfortable as was possible for the time being and, what was more, anyone coming down the basket chute would be sure to see Cadog and help him.

Rhidian had made up his mind. If he was to rescue his tribe before dawn, then time was short. He would take Cadog's pony, Eira. The boy felt no qualms about doing this. Cadog had, after all, offered to lend the pony. Although Rhidian knew that neither Cadog, nor the others, were likely to be pleased at his departure, he decided to leave them a message of sorts. To do this, he found a soft pebble and chalked a rough map of his intended route onto a flat piece of shale under the basket chute.

After making sure that Cadog was resting comfortably, Rhidian stepped out into the night air again. Eira was waiting just outside the cave. Fortunately for the boy, the pony was an altogether more friendly creature than Trojan had ever been; she stood patiently by while the powder barrels were loaded onto her back. Once this had been done, Rhidian set out along the path towards the river. He decided that, while still among the trees, he would lead Eira along on foot.

The boy realised that before he could proceed much further, it would be necessary for him to pass the *Woad*;

there was no way of avoiding it without making a long detour. For some reason, Rhidian felt disturbed by the prospect of passing that pool. His first night-time glimpse of it came when he spotted a shimmering image of the moon reflected through the tree trunks at the water's edge. As he walked along the river bank, with Eira at his side, the memory came flooding back of his earlier discussions with Aaron – discussions concerning the reputed spiritual properties of the pool and of its significance to followers of the Way. The water seemed calmer than before, its jade-green tinge by sunlight now muted into shades of grey; but it was still not the sort of place where Rhidian would have wished to take a plunge.

Now he realised what it was that had made him reluctant to pass this pool again; for it represented his failure to take that step into the water – that step of faith that Aaron had urged upon him. The boy was already convinced that the people of the Gwenfo tribe, and their friends, worshipped a most powerful God. After all, hadn't it been Aaron himself who had prophesied, in the name of this God, the disaster that would engulf Rhidian's tribe? Yet despite this, the boy could not see how immersing himself in a pool of water, as the pedlar would have had him do, could possibly solve his immediate problems. All the same, just for luck, Rhidian knelt down and dipped his hand in the water. Then he picked himself up and turned to leave.

As he did so, he almost collided with something else he had come across earlier in the day: the rock with the picture of Jesus on it. Rhidian stared at the painting. Like the pool, its natural colouring would not be visible again until daybreak; but the expression was still there in all its fullness. So too was the glistening effect of the wet paint.

Rhidian climbed into Eira's saddle and, from the *Woad*, set off in a southerly direction, following the paths that ran beside the Towy River. Cadog had been right about the pony; she was steady and predictable in her movements, qualities that Rhidian certainly appreciated after his unfortunate experiences with Trojan. The boy vowed that, in future, he would ride only Cambrian mountain ponies; Valeria would be welcome to keep her proud Arab stallion.

When the gradient of the river levelled out, Rhidian began to recognise his surroundings in the moonlight. As expected, he had now reached the northernmost part of the territory of his own tribe. The boy knew exactly where to turn next: the point at which the *Towy* was met by the stream of the *Llyfnant*. It was this stream which, if followed to its source, would lead to Beddau, the pass into the Vale of the Cothi.

When he reached the Llyfnant and started to proceed along it, Rhidian found his progress hampered. For one thing, the banks were often so overgrown with bushes that the boy had to move into the middle of the stream to avoid them and, even then, overhead branches would sometimes threaten to cause injury. In the end, Rhidian abandoned the course of the stream and took to higher

ground where the bushes and trees gave way to out-
crops of bracken. Eira's pace picked up immediately.
When the valley sides began to draw closer together
and the stream down below turned to a brook, Rhidian
knew that his destination could not be too far off.

Before long, the way ahead became funnelled into a
steep-sided ravine. Undoubtedly, this was the site of the
infamous landslide under which so many legionaries
had been crushed long ago. It was a forbidding landscape, laced with a mass of fallen boulders projecting
long shadows in the moonlight. Rhidian found it all too
easy to understand the Roman fear of this place; it was
unpleasant even for a Celt. The boy rode his way
uneasily through the rocks, fearful of what might be
lurking behind them. He tried not to let his eyes
wander too far to the left, or the right, in case he might
observe something that would be better left unnoticed.

It was a matter of some relief to Rhidian when he
emerged from the oppressive shadows of the ravine
onto the windswept expanse of the area beyond. He had
arrived at the pass. A wooden post had been driven into
the ground to mark the spot. Beyond it, the trail ahead
began to dip. Rhidian could just make out to his left a
large body of water, which he assumed was the reser-
voir of the Cothi Dam. To the boy's right, set back into
the hillside, was what he took to be the Mithras Temple
or, at least, the entrance to it – a sculpted granite arch
supported by heavy columns. There was no sign of any
movement on the outside of the Temple although, if

113

Cadog was right, the Ewenni tribe lay imprisoned somewhere within. The only way to discover the truth was to move in close.

Rhidian rode cautiously down to the side of the granite arch and then dismounted. He unloaded the barrels of Cambrian powder from Eira's back, placing them in a dry hole between some rocks. Leaving the pony tied to a tree, Rhidian took the torch he had brought with him and crept in under the columns of the Temple arch where he came up against a large oak door. It was a striking piece of craftsmanship with vast iron hinges and an enormous keyhole. In view of this last detail, Rhidian was a little surprised when he found that the door opened easily.

After satisfying himself that it was safe to proceed, the boy lit his torch although, unfortunately, its feeble flame illuminated little more than the immediate path ahead. A few paces inside the Temple, Rhidian came across another door. He was convinced that this must be the one that led to the catacombs, for it was made of iron like the one that Cadog had described. The boy pressed his ear against the metalwork and listened for signs of life, but all seemed quiet. He gingerly tapped on the door in the hope of arousing attention; there was no response. Perhaps the Ewenni were too far inside the catacombs to hear anything from the outside, or perhaps they were no longer in the Temple at all. It was impossible to tell without forcing an entry through the iron door. Rhidian had made up his mind to do just that, and to fetch the Cambrian powder for that purpose, when something quite unexpected happened: the Temple cavern suddenly came alive in a blaze of fire and light. The flames seemed to be coming from a series of lanterns hanging from above. Rhidian took them to be oil burners, not unlike the ones he had seen in the Dinas. The question was, who had set them alight and why?

However, it was what the burners revealed that most intrigued the boy. He could now see the Temple cavern properly. The walls were decorated with mysterious frescoes. There were images of a lion, a raven and a serpent. Towards the end of the cavern, a series of wooden steps led up to an altar; it was adorned with a set of horns which, no doubt, would once have belonged to a creature of considerable size.

Yet that was not all. Something had begun to emerge from behind the altar; it was the figure of a man. When the man reached the top of the altar steps, Rhidian finally realised the truth; he had come face to face with the very person he had hoped to avoid – Sulla.

CHAPTER EIGHT

# *The Unpardonable Sin*

Rhidian tried to make a dash for the door out of the Temple, but a couple of legionaries blocked the way.

"Do not be so hasty, young one," boomed Sulla. "We are always ready to receive those who show an interest in the ways of Mithras!"

Sulla walked calmly down the steps from the altar and stared at Rhidian with an air of curiosity.

"You have arrived here in time to witness a most important ceremony. No doubt, you were aware of that."

Rhidian shook his head.

"Either way," declared Sulla, "by the time this night is through, your education will be much improved."

"I am looking for the Ewenni."

"And why is that, boy?" asked Sulla, his face hardening. "Do you wish to become a slave, like one of them?"

At this, there was much laughter from the legionaries; but Rhidian remained stony-faced.

"Perhaps," suggested one of the men, "this lad is himself related to the Ewenni people."

Sulla gazed at Rhidian intently. "Well, boy? Is there any truth in this?"

"First, tell me where you have taken the tribe," came the reply.

"You are most persistent. Very well. Now that they have completed their work at the Dam, I have sent the Ewenni back to the Mines at Dolaucothi. There, they will be ready to begin extracting gold ore early in the morning."

At this news, Rhidian's heart sank. The boy now realised that his journey had been in vain. Sulla seemed to notice the change of mood immediately.

"Why, you really are of the Ewenni tribe, aren't you? I see it in your eyes. You must be the missing boy."

"Missing boy? What do you mean? You know nothing about me."

"Oh, but we do. One particular member of your tribe is a most co-operative fellow, quite unlike the others. He told us much that we wished to know – about many things. We know, for instance, that your name is Rhidian and that you were away from the Ewenni camp at the time when my men attacked it. It is also said that you may have been helped in the wilderness by a certain pedlar known as Aaron . . ."

At the mention of the pedlar's name, a flicker of recognition must have crossed Rhidian's face, for Sulla's tone suddenly became more threatening.

"Listen to me, boy! Keep away from that man, Aaron. His beliefs are dangerous."

"He's just a follower of the Way – that is all," said Rhidian, impatiently.

Sulla's face became filled with a look of savage intensity. "So, young Rhidian, Aaron is just a follower of the Way and that is all, is it? I sense that the old pedlar has already begun to poison your mind. No doubt, he has even attempted to convert you to his faith. That is unfortunate. If you are to be of use in the service of Mithras, we shall have to purge you of Aaron's influence."

Sulla barked an order at his legionaries, who promptly ran off to the back of the Temple cavern. They closed the main entrance and then opened the door to the catacombs. Meanwhile, Sulla climbed back up to the altar, raising the wooden steps behind him and leaving Rhidian standing in the middle of the cavern floor. Moments later came the sound of something unmistakable – the clatter of hooves on rock. Thinking that his pony, Eira, might be approaching, Rhidian turned round to look; but what he saw filled him with dread. Lumbering towards him was an enormous white bull.

Sulla folded his arms with grim satisfaction. "Observe, boy, our beast of sacrifice for the Ceremony of the White Bull. Since the moon is the symbol of the bull, it is our duty to celebrate on this night of the full moon. We had intended to slaughter the bull ourselves but, since you have yet to be initiated into the ways of Mithras, we would be honoured if you would perform the task for us."

"I want no part in your rituals," retorted Rhidian.

"Rituals, you say? Call them what you will. I merely suggest that you may wish to defend yourself."

Sulla promptly produced a set of javelins together with a sword. These items were thrown down to Rhidian. The sword was of a kind that the boy had never seen before. It was inlaid with jewels and bore an inscription on its handle.

However, even if he had been able to read the writing, Rhidian was in no position to inspect his new weapon closely, for the bull was already showing signs of aggression. Furthermore, the legionaries, who were now safely behind the door to the catacombs, had begun to throw stones at the creature, causing it to paw the ground with rage. Moments later, it charged straight across the cavern towards the only moving thing within reach – Rhidian.

Although terrified, the boy knew that his best chance of avoiding being hit was to hold his ground for a moment or two. This he did. Then, when the bull was just a few paces away, Rhidian leapt safely to one side. He ran across to the other side of the cavern, knowing that it would soon be necessary for him to repeat his move; except that this time he would defend himself properly.

When the bull came within range again, it was met with one of Rhidian's javelins. Unfortunately, this first missile glanced off the body of the creature and the boy was forced to jump out of the bull's path once more.

Rhidian's second javelin struck home, but it seemed to have little effect other than to enrage the animal still further. Time and time again, the boy managed to dodge out of the way of the beast hurtling towards him, but the relentless fury of the onslaught soon began to take its toll, leaving Rhidian bruised and close to exhaustion.

At one point, the boy stumbled and fell. Something dropped out of the folds of his tunic; he recognised it immediately – the vial of sleep-inducing resin that Aaron had given him. Rhidian had no time to lose, for the bull was pounding towards him once more, its nostrils steaming with exertion. The boy grabbed one of the javelins, smeared its tip with resin and, with a deft throw, managed to sink it into the bull's neck. The creature kept coming, regardless. After four more throws of the javelin, Rhidian's vial had almost run dry and, although the bull was becoming more sluggish in its movements, it was clear that the resin alone would not be enough to deter the creature.

Realising that Sulla would refuse to let him rest until the bull was dead, Rhidian picked up the sword he had been given and prepared to strike, positioning himself up against one of the cavern walls. When he was charged at again, Rhidian performed his well-tested manoeuvre of jumping to one side at the last moment. On this occasion, however, the bull could not stop in time to avoid colliding with the solid rock of the cavern wall. The impact left the beast dazed and vulnerable.

With his heart pounding, Rhidian mustered all his strength and drove his sword straight between the bull's shoulder blades. The creature staggered for just a moment and then fell to the ground – dead.

"A spirited performance, young Rhidian!" declared Sulla, gleefully, from his position by the altar. "In surviving this rite of initiation, you have earned yourself a place within the brotherhood of Mithras. Take up your weapons and march with us under the banner of the Bull!"

"No," replied Rhidian, throwing his sword defiantly to the ground. "If I am to become anything, I wish to become a follower of the Way, not a servant of Mithras."

"By which you mean, no doubt, that you wish to worship the Hebrew God, His Son, Jesus Christ, and the Holy Spirit, which is said to descend upon those who trust in Christ. I am afraid that it is too late for you to find favour with that strange Trinity, young Rhidian – your sins are too great."

"It is said that the sins of a person may be forgiven by God."

Sulla sneered. "Has it not also been said that he who blasphemes against the Holy Spirit *shall not* be forgiven?"

Rhidian froze. He knew that Sulla was scripturally correct from what Aaron had said earlier by the *Woad*; but why had the subject of blasphemy been mentioned at all? Rhidian was not aware that he had done anything, as such, that might fall within that description.

Sulla lowered the steps from the altar and then climbed down to the cavern floor. He picked up the sword that had been used to kill the bull, passed a finger along the blade, and then smeared the collected blood on Rhidian's forehead. The boy drew back in horror, much to Sulla's satisfaction.

"By taking up this sword as your weapon against the bull, you have become bonded to Mithras and separated from the God of the Hebrews. Allow me to read you the inscription which is plainly to be seen upon the sacrificial blade:

> *We, the redeemed from the slaying of the bull,*
> *In defiance of the blood of the Lamb,*
> *Our souls to Mithras do pledge in full,*
> *And the demons of the Dove we damn.*

"Observe, young Rhidian, the imagery of this inscription. Is Jesus Christ not signified by the Lamb, and the Holy Spirit, by the Dove. Is it not to be counted a blasphemy, by followers of the Way and their God, to associate the Dove, the Holy Spirit, with demons. Have you not, young Rhidian, by taking up the *Blade of Mithras* and its ethos, committed the one unpardonable sin – blasphemy against the Holy Spirit?"

As he heard these words, a terrible feeling of icy coldness passed through the pit of Rhidian's stomach. He knew, from what Aaron had told him, that blasphemy against the Holy Spirit was indeed the unpardonable sin; to commit it was to be condemned to eternal damnation. How Rhidian wished he had listened to Aaron's advice and stayed within the safe confines of the Dinas! In that place, there might still have been hope; but now, it was impossible for the boy ever to become a follower of the Way. He would be forever banished from God's presence. Even Aaron could do nothing for him now.

At that moment, although Rhidian was past caring, there was a disturbance outside the Temple doors and a group of legionaries marched in.

"What is it?" demanded Sulla, irritably.

"I bring news concerning Darius Maximus," said one of the legionaries. "He is approaching from the West."

"In that case, we must return to Luentinum at once to prepare for the next stage of our operation."

Sulla turned to Rhidian. "You will bow to Mithras in the end, boy, make no mistake! Until we return, you will remain here in the Temple."

The legionaries bound Rhidian to a pillar. Sulla then took his sword and pressed the blade lightly across the boy's forearm. It was enough to cause a slight wound although not a painful one. Sulla then took the vial of resin that the boy had been carrying and allowed the contents to drip into the wound. Rhidian put up a struggle, but the effort was pointless. Moments later, the boy lost consciousness and passed into a sleep troubled by dark visions.

# CHAPTER NINE

# Valeria Intervenes

For some time after Rhidian had left the Dinas, the remaining occupants of the High Hollow had slept on oblivious of developments elsewhere that night. Eventually, however, Valeria awoke to find that her friend was missing.

Taking care not to disturb anyone else, the girl searched through the Dinas until she discovered that the basket in the chute had been lowered. Guessing that Rhidian must have had some reason to wander out, Valeria raised the basket and used it to descend to the bottom of the chute. There she was greeted by Cadog, whom she recognised from the previous day.

At first, the injured man seemed greatly relieved to see Valeria, but his relief soon turned to dismay when he realised that the girl had come alone. Cadog had reason to feel disappointed; he knew that the basket-raising mechanism was no longer capable of lifting the weight of a person back to the top of the chute unless someone was there to pull the rope in from above. Since no-one had accompanied Valeria, the chances were that it would be impossible to re-enter the Dinas until someone else arrived at daybreak.

The matter of most concern to Valeria herself, however, was the question of what had happened to Rhidian. When Cadog explained that the boy had set out for the Mithras Temple, Valeria was greatly alarmed. She decided that she had to try to find her friend. To do so, she would take Trojan, for the stallion was still harnessed where it had earlier been left by Aaron – just outside the entrance to the Dinas. After making sure that Cadog was resting comfortably, and that he knew what to tell the others, Valeria bade the man farewell and set off in pursuit of Rhidian.

Although the girl was not familiar with the route to the Cothi Pass, she knew that it would be necessary to journey alongside the Towy River a short distance and then branch off to follow the course of the Llyfnant until its source was reached. In finding her way, Valeria was greatly assisted, as Rhidian had been, by the light of the moon. Here and there along the way, the moon could also be glimpsed by reflection in the waterlogged, hoof-imprinted mud of the river banks, confirmation to Valeria that Rhidian had indeed passed that same way.

When she arrived at the Mithras Temple, the girl found Rhidian still bound to the pillar where Sulla had left him. Valeria guessed that her friend might have been drugged in some way, for his appearance reminded her of the condition of the two legionaries – the ones whom Rhidian had shot with his resin-tainted darts back at the Ford.

Not wishing to remain at the Temple for longer than was absolutely necessary, Valeria lifted her friend onto Trojan's back. Then, after tying the boy firmly in position behind her, she set off on the return journey to the Dinas with Eira, the pony, in tow. Fortunately, there had been no sign of Sulla, and Valeria made good progress, arriving at the edge of the *Woad* just as the moon's glow began to give way to the glimmer of an approaching dawn.

Valeria dismounted and rolled out a blanket that had been left slung across Eira's back. She then placed the blanket around Rhidian's shoulders and carried him over to a nearby patch of leaves in among some rocks beside the pool. Once there, Valeria decided to try rousing Rhidian from his slumbers and so she gave him a sharp prod or two. It was this prodding which eventually woke the boy although it was some time before he opened his eyes.

"My word, Rhid," said Valeria, trying to sound cheerful, "you've certainly been in the wars. With all those bruises, anyone would think you've just come back from the wrong side of Hadrian's Wall!"

"Be serious, Valeria," groaned Rhidian. "Where am I?"

"Where you should have been all along," replied the girl, a little reproachfully. "Next time you decide to set out on a moonlight expedition, let me know first."

Rhidian tried to elbow himself into an upright position, but soon fell back, exhausted.

"It's not safe here," he breathed. "Sulla said that he would be coming back to this valley at the first opportunity. We'd better warn the others."

"I only wish we could," sighed Valeria, "but until someone in the High Hollow wakes up and realises we've gone, there is no way of getting inside the Dinas. That basket-raising mechanism of yours isn't working properly."

Rhidian buried his face in his hands. "I had forgotten about the basket; so it's still not working, then. I'm not much of a Master of the Elements, after all, am I?"

"Most inventions have their flaws at first," said Valeria, trying to console her friend. "I'm sure you'll have that basket fixed just as soon as you're well enough."

"I'll never be well enough," muttered Rhidian, miserably. "It's too late for that."

"Too late? What are you talking about, Rhid?"

"If everything that happened in the Mithras Temple was real, then I'm doomed. The God of the Gwenfo tribe will never forgive me for what I have done. My sin is unpardonable."

"Nonsense, Rhid. Followers of the Way believe that their God may forgive *any* sin."

"Not this one; it's called blasphemy against the Holy Spirit."

Valeria looked puzzled. "That doesn't sound such a terrible thing to have done."

"You don't understand; it is condemned in the Scriptures."

"Well, I'm sure that, when we see them, either Aaron or Eifiona will have the answer to your problem."

"Oh, I do hope so," said the boy, fervently.

At Valeria's insistence, Rhidian then described most of what had happened at the Temple. Somehow, the act of doing this, with Valeria commenting along the way, seemed to cheer the boy up considerably. Even so, he still appeared desperately tired, no doubt owing to the continuing effect of the resin in his blood.

Valeria put her arms around her friend and gave him an affectionate hug. His cheeks were pale and he had begun to shiver in the damp chill of the morning twilight air. Gently, Valeria drew Rhidian's blanket up over his shoulders for extra warmth.

"Something you were murmuring in your sleep has been bothering me, Rhid," said the girl. "I heard it a number of times – that '*Darius Maximus is coming*', or something like that."

Rhidian frowned. "Those are the words of the centurion – the one who reported to Sulla just before I lost consciousness."

"Where is Darius supposed to be now?"

"You know him?"

"He's a friend of my father's; or, at least, he was. They hadn't seen each other for a while. Darius is a good soldier – well respected by his men. Just the sort of person you would want on your side."

129

"Well, it looks as if Sulla wants Darius on *his* side. He's hoping to meet him at the fort."

"The fort at Dolaucothi? Luentinum? When?"

"This very morning. Darius is approaching from the West."

Valeria rose to her feet. "If what you say is true, there's no time to lose. I must try to intercept Darius before he reaches the fort. Perhaps I can persuade him to side with us against Sulla. It's our best hope of stopping the Decurio at the moment, anyway. What do you say, Rhid?"

Rhidian did not respond. When Valeria looked across at her friend, she noticed that he had fallen asleep again. It seemed that the effect of the resin in Rhidian's blood had yet to work its way out of his system.

The boy's condition left Valeria in a dilemma. While she truly wished to stay with her friend and assist his recovery, the girl also knew that, in the long run, there was only one sure way to help Rhidian and the others – Sulla's plans had to be thwarted. In order to do this, it would be necessary to leave Rhidian at the Dinas, for the boy clearly was in no state to travel.

Valeria left Rhidian where he lay for a few moments and climbed up to the entrance cave of the Dinas. There the girl explained her situation to Cadog, asking him to take care of Rhidian until someone else from within the Dinas came along. After expressing some frustration at the fact that his own injuries prevented him from doing more to help, Cadog reluctantly agreed to the plan. He hobbled out of the entrance cave, with Valeria's help, and sat himself down in a position where he would best be able to keep watch over Rhidian and observe the area where someone coming out of the Dinas would emerge.

When all was ready, Valeria approached the sleeping figure of Rhidian and gave him one final kiss on the forehead. Then the girl untied Trojan, the stallion, swung herself into the saddle and rode off into the dim mists of the dawn.

# CHAPTER TEN

# A Face Upon the Waters

Shortly after Valeria had left the Dinas, Rhidian stirred again. He finally came to when a sudden gust of wind blew in from across the pool, dropping its leafy load on the boy's blanket. Still in a weakened state, Rhidian slowly pulled himself to his feet and peered at his surroundings. Little seemed to have changed since his last awakening; the orange glow gathering on the eastern horizon had yet to overcome the shadowy gloom lingering still beneath the trees.

Rhidian looked around for Valeria, but neither she nor Cadog were to be seen. Thinking that his friends might be somewhere nearby, the boy took a few faltering steps towards the edge of the pool, calling as he went; there was no response.

Still feeling weary, Rhidian knelt down beside the pool, cupped his hands in the water and washed his face. As he did so, he caught a glimpse of his own reflection staring back at him from below. It was then that he noticed a dark streak running diagonally from his left temple to his right. For a moment, he couldn't quite make out what it was; but then the truth dawned on the boy. He was staring at the mark of the bull's blood – the blood that had been smeared on his forehead by Sulla.

To Rhidian, it was a terrifying sight, a hideous reminder of his involvement in the blasphemous rituals at the Mithras Temple. Hurriedly, the boy splashed some more water on his face in an attempt to remove the blood, but the mark simply refused to come off. Rhidian's worst fears had been realised. If the mark could not be removed, it could surely mean only one thing: that Rhidian's use of the *Blade of Mithras*, with its diabolical inscription, had indeed been a blasphemy against the Holy Spirit. Why else should the conse- crated waters of the pool, the very instrument of the Holy Spirit, fail to cleanse away the blood?

As these thoughts raced through his mind, some- thing else occurred to Rhidian. Hadn't Aaron spoken of the dangerous properties of the pool and of its reputa- tion as a place of judgment for agents of the evil one? If Rhidian's participation in the sacrifice of the bull made him just such an agent, then the pool could be his death trap. As soon as this possibility occurred to him, Rhidian leapt away from the water's edge and began to back off into the woods.

Of all the sins he could have committed, thought the boy, desperately, why was it that his sin had to have been the unpardonable one? If it had been any other, he could simply have asked the God of the Gwenfo tribe for forgiveness. As things were, that possibility was forever closed to Rhidian and, with it, the chance of his ever becoming a follower of the Way.

Still edging his way backwards, Rhidian unexpectedly came into contact with an object. He spun round immediately and noticed that he was standing next to something he had seen earlier – the rock with the painting of Jesus on it. The boy had forgotten it was there. Now that the moon had disappeared, the shadows surrounding the image were positioned differently from before and it was no longer possible to make out the hands and face of the figure on the rock. As a result, Rhidian's attention was drawn to the area immediately below the painting and on something now visible there which the boy had previously missed: a set of symbols. They seemed strangely familiar, but some moments passed before Rhidian realised what they represented. With trembling hands, he reached inside his tunic and drew out the strip of parchment that Valeria had given him the day before. It was as he had suspected – the symbols on the rock and the writing on the parchment were identical; and, since Rhidian remembered Valeria's translation of the words on the parchment, he also knew the meaning of the rock symbols:

*The LORD does not see as man sees;*
*for man looks at the outward appearance,*
*but the LORD looks at the heart.*

As he stood there, staring at the rock, a thought struck Rhidian. Could it be, he wondered, that of all the passages of Scripture, this seemingly insignificant one held an answer to the problem of the unpardonable sin? Somehow, it seemed too much to hope. Yet if the unpardonable sin had nothing to do with the passage, what sort of sinner would find comfort in its words? Perhaps one who, though intending no wrong, had nevertheless done something which, to men, had the appearance of being a sin. These were precisely the circumstances in which Rhidian seemed to find himself; for, although the boy had used the *Blade of Mithras*, with its chilling inscription, he had done so only to defend himself against the bull and not with the intention of committing blasphemy.

Was it therefore possible, the boy now wondered, if the words visible on the rock were a sign from the God of the Gwenfo tribe that Rhidian had not committed the unpardonable sin and that it was still possible to become a follower of the Way?

For the first time since he had left the Mithras Temple, a real sense of hope had returned to Rhidian. He walked slowly back to the edge of the pool and looked into the water again. Earlier, the blood mark on his forehead had held the boy's attention completely. Now he was able to take in the whole of his reflection without distraction.

Reassuring though this was, somehow the sight of that shimmering image in the water began to make the boy feel deeply ashamed of himself – ashamed of all the wrong turns he had made in the previous few days. It was as if, now free of the fear of the *unpardonable* sin, Rhidian was now being made aware of all his other sins – the *pardonable* ones – such as his feelings of anger towards Valeria over Trojan, the stallion; his insistence on preparing Cambrian powder against Aaron's advice; and, most of all, his failure to become a follower of the Way when the opportunity had arisen the day before. Rhidian knew, then and there, that all these wrong things he had done needed to be put right; but how was it to be achieved?

Slowly, but instinctively, Rhidian rose to his feet and took a few paces into the woods. Then he turned round again, prayed to the God of the Gwenfo tribe that his sins might be forgiven and, with a running jump, hurled himself quite deliberately into the foaming, grey waters of the pool.

Down into the cold depths he plunged until, eventually, he struck the bottom of the pool. As he did so, he became caught up among the rocks of the river bed. Fortunately, Rhidian was soon able to shake himself free although not without dragging away something that had become stuck to his feet – it felt like part of a submerged root system.

Rhidian pushed himself off from the bottom of the pool and tried to swim upwards as best he could. Powerful undercurrents threatened to pull him off course but, as the orange glow from the dawn above grew stronger, the boy knew he was rising. By the time he broke the surface of the pool, he was gasping for air, but managed to haul himself over to the river bank with the help of an overhanging branch.

As the boy emerged from the water, the orb of the sun began to rise above the mountain ranges far off on the eastern horizon. Diffused by shades of orange and yellow, and the dust of the willow herb, a kindly swathe of light grazed the forest floor where Rhidian stood, bathing him in a glow of sublime warmth. The boy was overwhelmed with a sense of peace and well-being. Yet he also felt within himself a fresh and boundless energy. Rhidian knew at once that his sins had indeed been forgiven, and that he had been made as new, just as surely as he now saw in his surroundings the renewing hand of the Creator.

Rhidian gazed with fascination at the wispy vapours drifting delicately between the boughs, freed from watery globules by the simmering shafts of the sun. Was this, the boy wondered, what it had been like in the beginning when the world was formed and primordial mists watered the earth? Perhaps so; and yet Rhidian was aware that all was not now as it might have been in this garden of the wilds, something that seemed to have found its expression in the aroma of decaying leaves left abandoned from the gusts of early autumn.

In the midst of this garden of what once had been, and yet might be again, lay a symbol of that which had bridged the divide between the two: the rock bearing the image of Jesus upon it. Yet now, unlike before, the true nature and extent of the picture was revealed in all the fullness of its colour. The glistening effect of what had once been fresh paint, however, now seemed to have disappeared. Rhidian reached out to touch the image, but he soon drew his hand back sharply. He felt certain that the spot he had made contact with was still wet. Sure enough, deposited on his fingers were the distinct traces of moist, red paint – paint which represented the blood from the wounds on the hands of Christ.

The boy dropped to his knees beneath the painting, closed his eyes and offered a prayer of thanks to his Saviour, Jesus, the Lamb of God, by whose Blood the blood of the bull, and the dominion of Mithras, had been overcome.

For some time, Rhidian remained in a state of quiet contemplation beneath the image on the rock. He was taken by surprise when he opened his eyes to discover that Aaron was standing nearby. Influenced, no doubt, by Rhidian's soaking condition, the pedlar immediately offered to lend the boy his cloak. The offer was gratefully taken up just as soon as Rhidian had managed to remove his dripping clothes. Whatever creature had lost its skin in the making of Aaron's cloak, thought the boy, it had bequeathed a most effective barrier against the cold.

"You were right to warn me of the traps of the devil," said the boy, uncomfortably. "I should never have left the Dinas on my own."

The pedlar smiled. "Do not trouble yourself too greatly, my friend. Perhaps my counsel of yesterday was less wise than it appeared at the time – for, by all accounts, it would seem that you have emerged much the stronger for your encounter with Sulla."

"Then you already know something of what happened at the Mithras Temple?"

"Indeed I do – Cadog has told me a great deal about it; but he did not say that you had responded to the Lord's calling and become a follower of the Way. For that knowledge, I had to rely on the evidence of my own eyes – your movements here beside the pool were unmistakable."

"After what I did at the Mithras Temple, do you think it was foolish of me to dive into the pool? After all, I suppose that if I had blasphemed against the Holy Spirit, and committed the unpardonable sin, these hallowed waters might have closed over me for good."

Aaron placed a reassuring hand on Rhidian's shoulder. "It would certainly be as well to be accompanied by someone before venturing again into such turbulent currents. Yet, for you, Rhidian, the dangers of this pool are merely of the bodily kind, not the spiritual. From what Cadog has told me, I do not believe you were ever at risk of committing the unpardonable sin at the Mithras Temple. You were tricked into doing what you did. Besides, it seems that you never even uttered the words of the inscription upon the *Blade of Mithras*. You merely used the weapon to defend yourself against the bull. The Lord knows that, in your heart, you intended no blasphemy. He will not hold you to account for the way things may have appeared; for it is written: 'The LORD does not see as man sees . . .' "

"For man looks at the outward appearance," recited Rhidian, confidently, "but the LORD looks at the heart."

Aaron seemed startled by the nature of the interruption. "For a newcomer to the faith, your knowledge of the Scriptures is extraordinary."

The boy smiled to himself. It had plainly not occurred to the pedlar that the passage of Scripture in question might be the *only* one that Rhidian knew. The boy was wondering whether he ought to point this out when Aaron began speaking again.

"To welcome you into the company of the faithful," said the pedlar, "I have something here for you."

Aaron reached for an object that he had been wearing around his neck. It was a pendant, of a sort, about the size of a large, circular coin, with unusual markings spaced at regular intervals around the edge. Balanced on a pivot at the centre of the object was a short, tapering filament, having the shape of an arrow.

"The arrow upon this pendant," said the pedlar, "is made from a type of mineral known as a lodestone. One end of such a stone, when freely suspended, normally will turn towards the north. In the case of this pendant, it is the pointed end of the arrow filament which indicates the north. Therefore, if ever you are travelling in the wilderness, and you know which way you should be heading – let us say, towards the west, for instance – then line up the direction in which the arrow is pointing with the mark for *north* on the edge of the pendant and, while ensuring that this setting does not change, walk in a straight line in your chosen direction, as indicated by the marking on the edge of the pendant.

"Over the course of my wanderings, I have found this lodestone to be of valuable assistance on many an occasion. Therefore, as one follower of the Way to another, I commend it to you."

With that, the pedlar took the pendant and hung it around Rhidian's neck.

"If you no longer have a lodestone yourself," objected the boy, "how will you continue to be able to find your way in these parts?"

Aaron laughed. "When a man has walked the Cambrian mountains as often as I have, he develops a sense of direction better than that of any lodestone. Therefore, my friend, receive the pendant with my blessing. I can think of no better gift for a young follower of the Way than one which offers the means of keeping a straight course – as straight as is the course of the Saviour Himself."

Rhidian thanked the pedlar for his unusual gift and assured him that it would be put to good use when the boy needed to venture into the mountains once more. It was this thought of journeying in the mountains that suddenly reminded Rhidian of Valeria. Where had the girl gone? Not so long before, she had been at Rhidian's side. The boy was shocked when Aaron explained what had happened – that Valeria had set out on her own for Dolaucothi. If only she had waited for just a little longer, thought the boy, she could have taken someone with her. After all, Rhidian himself needed to reach the Mines to rescue his tribe; now the boy might have to rescue Valeria as well. As Aaron pointed out, however, neither he nor Rhidian could do much to help Valeria if they stayed beside the pool. It was time to regroup with the Gwenfo tribe and to consult with them about what could best be done next.

When the pedlar turned to walk back towards the Dinas, Rhidian made as if to follow, but he tripped over something stretched across the ground. On closer inspection, it turned out to be a length of rope, of the sort made from strands of twisted vine.

"From its condition," observed the pedlar, "I should say that, until very recently, this rope has been lying submerged beneath the water – and for some considerable time."

"Of course!" exclaimed Rhidian. "It became attached to my feet when I was trapped for a short time at the bottom of the pool. At least, it *felt* like a rope, or something similar. I had almost forgotten about that moment."

Aaron rubbed his chin, thoughtfully, and then began to pull in the part of the rope left hidden within the pool. Owing to some hidden obstruction beneath the water, it required the combined strength of both Aaron and Rhidian to complete the task. Rather to their disappointment, however, all they found at the other end of the rope was a rotten piece of wood. The only remarkable thing about it was its unnaturally flat and oval shape, a sign perhaps that it had been man-made at some point in the past.

"No doubt, Eifiona, or one of the others, will be able to tell us what the object is," said Aaron, looking baffled. "Come, Rhidian, it is time we put your clothes to dry. Though my cloak sits well upon your shoulders, I shall not be disappointed to see it returned to me! The air is turning colder. Mark my words, there will be snow in the mountains before this day is through."

The lifting mechanism over the basket chute, as Rhidian soon discovered, appeared to be operating normally once more. Whatever had caused the previous fault had now righted itself. In any event, the mechanism transported its load up into the heights of the Dinas without faltering and, before long, Rhidian and Aaron were back in the High Hollow where most of the members of the Gwenfo tribe were huddled in earnest debate around the fire.

News had already reached them of the events of the previous night and, as soon as they saw Rhidian, they gathered round in a spirit of sympathetic curiosity and sat him down in prime position near the hearth. Eifiona poured the boy a warm, sweet drink, tasting of wild berries, from a flagon suspended over the fire-place.

Even the gruff-sounding Gwion offered Rhidian a leg from the roasted rabbit he happened to be eating.

After Rhidian had responded to a frenzy of questions on all sides about his expedition to the Mithras Temple, and his later, extraordinary experiences back at the pool, the conversation in the High Hollow inevitably turned to the mysterious piece of wood that Aaron and the boy had brought in from outside the Dinas and which now lay drying off for all to see upon the hearth.

When he heard that the find had come from the pool, Iago, the lamplighter, seemed especially intrigued. He took the object into his hands and examined it carefully, growing more and more excited by the moment. Finally, he looked up at the expectant faces around him.

"It's my belief," he stated, "that what we have here is nothing less than the remains of a *cherub*."

"A *cherub*?" inquired Eifiona, looking puzzled. "Is that not the name given to a certain order of the angels of heaven?"

"So it is said. However, the angel to which this wooden object belongs is not of the heavenly host; it is entirely of worldly origin – one of Towser's flying craft, to be precise."

"You mean, Towser actually *made* one of those infernal things he always spoke of – a set of wings for jumping off the summit of the Dinas?"

"Yes indeed. Naturally, he wished to keep the project quiet until everything had been properly tested. He let *me* in on the secret, though. I helped him construct the machine, but it crashed on its first flight. Although Towser jumped out before the wings hit the ground, we never did find the wreckage. Now I know why! It must have plunged straight into that pool and wedged itself at the bottom."

"But how can you be sure that what you have in your hand is from Towser's machine?"

"I recognise the words carved on the underside of the wood. Towser had them placed at the tail-end of his machine:

*"And He rode upon a cherub, and flew;*
*He flew upon the wings of the wind."*

"Ah yes," murmured Eifiona. "That passage is taken from one of the psalms of Scripture, although I don't suppose the psalmist had flying machines in mind when he composed his words! Still, at least we seem to have discovered where Towser found the idea of calling his machine a *cherub* . . ."

Eifiona had broken off her sentence in mid-flow. She was staring towards the passageway that led into the High Hollow with a look of trepidation on her face. When Rhidian followed her gaze, he could see why. One of the younger members of the tribe was standing at the entrance of the cavern, looking dishevelled and out of breath. When he spoke, the urgency in the tone of his voice was unmistakable.

"We're surrounded! There must be dozens of them

146

down there in the valley."

"Dozens of what?" asked everyone at once.

"Romans!" came the reply.

# CHAPTER ELEVEN

# The Decurio Unmasked

After leaving Rhidian at the Dinas, Valeria decided that the best way for her to reach Dolaucothi was to return to the Mithras Temple and then proceed through the Vale of the Cothi beyond. For the first part of her journey, therefore, the girl was able to follow a riverside route that was familiar to her from earlier that morning. She urged her horse onwards at as rapid a pace as she dared; for if Darius was to be intercepted before his arrival at the fort, there was no time to lose. Although she did not expect to see any legionaries before reaching the Mithras Temple, the girl nevertheless remained on her guard and, as she approached the Beddau Pass, kept well within the cover of the rocks and trees that lined the way.

Once clear of the Temple, Valeria passed into the woods running alongside another structure of Roman origin: the Cothi Dam. It was easy enough to spot in the light of the rising sun; but the sound was particularly noticeable. Indeed, it almost seemed as if all the rains of the season had found their way into the dam, such was the torrent crashing down across the overflow and into the river bed downstream. A large mound of leaves nearby seemed to provide some evidence that the Ewenni tribe had indeed been clearing debris from the site, as Cadog and Rhidian had earlier reported.

The girl pressed on down the valley, following a duct that channelled some of the water away from the retaining wall of the dam and on towards the mines. After progressing along the duct for a mile or so, Valeria caught a glimpse of what she knew must be Luentinum – the fort at Dolaucothi. Veering off to the right, she avoided the territory immediately surrounding the mines and worked her way through a densely wooded area until she came out above the road leading west of the fort.

Valeria was about to head out towards the road when she noticed that someone was already on it – many people, in fact – most of them on horseback but with a number of others attending to some wagons being drawn along behind. At the front of the column could be seen a distinctive-looking standard. It was the one used by Darius and his cohort; of this, Valeria was confident. She was less confident, however, of what to do next. The original plan had been to meet Darius a little further to the west and away from Luentinum. Yet now, since the Tribune had moved faster than expected, Valeria was faced with the prospect of having to meet the man much closer to the fort. It was an uncomfortable position to be in, but the alternatives were few. To wait might mean never again having as good an opportunity to speak alone with Darius and his men.

Valeria had made up her mind. Leaving her horse tied to the trunk of an old oak, she broke her cover and set out over the open meadow which led down to the road. The distance to be crossed was further than the girl had expected. By the time she drew close to the road, the front of the procession – where Darius was presumably positioned – had moved past. Rather to Valeria's surprise, none of the legionaries seemed to recognise her. She certainly recognised some of *them*. Perhaps they assumed that a specimen as wild in appearance as Valeria had now become could not possibly be the girl they remembered. In any event, they mostly ignored her presence.

By this point, Valeria was running alongside the rear of the moving column, trying to catch up with the front; but before she was able to do so, she suddenly noticed a separate group of men approaching the column from the opposite direction – from the fort. With a shock, the girl recognised one of the men in particular: it was Sulla. He had evidently decided not to wait for Darius to march past the fort but had chosen, instead, to come out and greet his new arrival.

Valeria stopped short. If she continued onwards, she would walk straight into Sulla's hands. However, to turn back across the open meadow, in full view of anyone who chose to look, would also have been undesirable. There was only one thing to be done. Valeria turned and ran back towards the rear of the column. In this, she was assisted, as before, by the fact that none of the legionaries seemed to be taking much notice of her. Why should they? Unlike Sulla, they had no reason to be on the lookout for a fugitive.

So it was that when Valeria reached the last wagon of the column, she was able to hop into it unnoticed and hide among some boxes that lay within. The situation was hardly ideal, but it would have to do. With any luck, the column would soon be past Luentinum and on its way to Alabum. That, felt the girl, would be the moment to speak with Darius.

Valeria had scarcely had time to move into position when the procession drew to a halt. It seemed likely that this was due to Sulla's presence up ahead; but whatever the nature of the conversation which must have been taking place there, the wagon in which Valeria was hiding soon began to creak forwards once more. Through the gaps between the boxes in the wagon, the girl was able to make out the ramparts of Luentinum.

Much to her consternation, however, instead of continuing along the road leading east towards Alabum, the column soon began to approach the fort itself; Darius and his men had clearly decided to enter the gates. Not that Valeria now had any realistic choice but to stay where she was at that moment – Sulla's sentries on the walls of the fort certainly would have spotted any attempt at escape. Nevertheless, Valeria now faced a situation she had not anticipated just moments before. She would simply have to try and remain hidden until a suitable opportunity to meet Darius presented itself. After all, there was always the chance that the Tribune would leave the fort again very soon, perhaps after taking on some supplies.

Darius's men proceeded straight through the gates of the fort and dispersed themselves around the compound. Valeria eventually found herself positioned next to the stables from where she was able to observe much of the activity taking place around her. By the look of things, many of the legionaries were heading for the refectory to find food, leaving their horses to drink from the water troughs dotted around the fort.

Yet it was the whereabouts of Darius that most concerned Valeria. She finally spotted the Tribune walking in the opposite direction from that of his men; he was heading towards the Prefect's Villa – a most sumptuous place of residence, so it was said, although Valeria had never been allowed inside. The villa was usually occupied by whoever happened to be in command of the fort. At Luentinum, the name of that person, as Valeria well knew, would be Sulla. From the girl's point of view, therefore, to walk into the villa was likely to be an undertaking of considerable risk. However, for the chance of speaking with Darius, Valeria was willing to try anything. In any case, the girl would not necessar-

153

ily be in a safer position if she remained where she was.

Valeria carefully climbed out of the wagon in which she had been hiding. Stealthily, and taking great pains not to be seen, the girl wove her way from building to building across the compound until she reached the entrance of the Prefect's Villa. Slowly, she pushed the door open and gazed in awe at the ornate hallway beyond. There were sculpted marble figures set into the walls and a mosaic-tiled floor into which had been sunk a set of pipes to accommodate a version of that most civilised of Roman inventions: the hypocaust heating system. Indeed, it was the effect of the hypocaust that Valeria noticed most of all as she stepped out of the cold and into the controlled warmth of the villa.

The girl crept across the hallway and peered into one of the rooms beyond. Like the rest of the villa, the room was grand in appearance with an arched roof and hanging frescoes; but it was evidently intended to act as a place for dining, for in the centre of the room was a table loaded with many unusual Roman delicacies – spiced buns, stuffed dormice and the like.

Valeria had just moved over to inspect the table more closely when she heard a noise coming from somewhere nearby.

"And who might you be?" came a voice from behind the door. "This is no place for youngsters."

The door swung round to reveal a rather surprised-looking Darius seated on a couch.

"Don't you remember me?" asked Valeria, hopefully.

The Tribune seemed at a loss for words.

"You know my father," added the girl.

Darius clasped his hands together. "Of course! You're the daughter of Trophimus, aren't you?"

Valeria nodded firmly.

"Well, I should be careful if I were you," continued the Tribune, eyeing Valeria's tousled appearance. "You might be mistaken for being a child of the tribes. Where's your father? Isn't he here?"

"I wish he was. He wouldn't put up with any nonsense from that man Sulla."

"Oh – him. He wants to see me, by the way. Considering he's a decurio and an inspector of mines, Sulla strikes me as quite a reasonable fellow."

"No. You're wrong," said Valeria, earnestly. "He means the people of this area no good at all. Can't you order him to leave?"

Darius shifted uncomfortably in his seat. "Sulla is of higher rank than me – and your father, come to that. I would want to see an order sealed by Constantius himself before acting against an imperial inspector of mines. Besides, what is so bad about this Sulla?"

"He attacked an innocent tribe in the Towy Valley."

"Then I daresay he won't be the first Roman to have done such a thing. Maybe there was good reason for the attack. It is impossible to say without knowing more . . ."

At that moment, Valeria heard the sound of someone opening the main door of the villa.

"That'll be Sulla now," whispered Darius, urgently.

155

"It was he who told me to wait in here."

Valeria realised immediately that she could not hope to leave the villa without being seen – for there was only one door out of the room she was in and it led straight back into the hallway. In panic, and pleading with Darius not to betray her presence, Valeria dived for cover behind a nearby wooden chest. It was hardly the safest place to hide, but there was little choice.

No sooner had the girl hidden herself than she heard Sulla speaking. His commanding voice would have been recognisable to Valeria anywhere. After greeting Darius, the Decurio invited his guest to take whatever he wished of the considerable quantity of food laid out on the table. From her position behind the chest, Valeria was just able to make out Darius starting rather gingerly on a grape or two.

"Tell me," began Sulla, between mouthfuls of ham, "what is your opinion of our new system of mining inspections?"

Darius hesitated.

"You may speak freely," added Sulla, leaning back in his seat.

"Well, sir, it is said in the ranks – but not by me, you understand – that these inspections of the mines do no good at all."

"Why so?"

"Take these diggings at Dolaucothi, for instance. The best of the seams were mined years ago. That's why the people around here have a saying: '*You'd sooner find a yellow nugget in the river than a speck of gold down the mines'."*

"If what you say is true – and I have yet to determine that it is – then it would be desirable, would it not, to locate an alternative source of precious metal?"

"Desirable – yes; but such a source has yet to be found."

"Have you not heard of the hidden vein of gold known as the *Cambrian Lode*?"

"You should be aware, sir, that few of us believe in its existence."

"Be that as it may, what if I were to tell you that I had information in my possession which might lead to the discovery of the *Lode*?"

"That would be a piece of information worth investigating."

"Indeed so. In fact, I would like you and your men to assist me in just such an investigation. The first step would be to capture the tribe which holds the secret of the gold."

Darius looked dubious. "So there is a tribe, is there? That makes my position difficult."

"Why difficult?" asked Sulla, a little irritation creeping into his voice. "An inspector of mines, such as myself, is entitled to receive the assistance of any Roman forces based in or around an establishment under investigation."

"Provided," said Darius, slowly, "that the inspector's request for assistance relates directly to his investiga-

157

tion. An attack against one of the hill tribes may or may not fall within that description. Before undertaking anything, I should like some indication from my superiors here in Cambria that the course of action you propose would be acceptable."

From her hiding place behind the chest, Valeria almost expected Sulla to explode with rage at this challenge to his authority from Darius. In fact, the Decurio simply smiled and then calmly proceeded to remove a small document from a pouch on his belt.

"I believe this may clarify the matter in hand," said Sulla, pointing to the document. He then began to read its contents out loud:

*"Those in positions of authority in the Cambrian Region are reminded of their duty to co-operate fully with the officials of the Imperial Inspectorate of Mines. Until further notice, the instructions of such officials are to be obeyed insofar as the carrying out of those instructions may lead, either directly or indirectly, to improvements in the yield of mining operations."*

Darius seemed a little puzzled. "Might I ask whose name appears beneath those words?"

"See for yourself, my friend," said Sulla, handing the document over. "I believe you will recognise the seal; it belongs to one Baronius Flavius – a most favoured adviser in the court of Constantius."

Darius examined the document carefully and then

placed it on the table, expressionless. "It would seem that I am yours to command."

"You do not sound . . . pleased."

Darius sighed. "It has taken a great deal of time for us to earn the trust of the local tribes. I am not sure that it would be wise to squander that trust over a vein of gold that may not even exist."

"Times change, my friend. If we are to sustain the Empire through these troubled days, we shall require all the gold we can lay our hands on. Naturally, any such precious metal tends to provide its own reward to those who prove instrumental in discovering it . . ."

"Very well. What is it that you wish me to do?"

"In the higher reaches of the Vale of the Towy there lies a certain prominent hill – a natural fortress of sorts – shaped in the likeness of a volcano."

"I have heard of it."

"Then take your men and surround this hill, for I have it on good authority that somewhere within its mysterious caverns lies the home of the Gwenfo tribe – the very same folk who hold the secret of the *Cambrian Lode*."

"If these people live where you say they do, I do not see how we can prise their secret from them easily. It may not be enough merely to lay siege to their hideout; we may have to storm it."

"Leave that to me. All you need do is to stop the Gwenfo tribe from escaping until I arrive with Diophantus."

Darius frowned. "Did you say Diophantus? Would

that be Diophantus Severus from Dacia? Isn't he the man who was responsible for setting ablaze an entire city because he suspected the folk there of harbouring a certain rebel leader?"

"Perhaps you are thinking of someone else," said Sulla, quickly. "The Diophantus I know is an effective commander, to be sure, but he is no more ruthless than I am myself."

"Where is Diophantus now?" asked Darius, warily.

"I received news just yesterday that he has landed off the south coast of Cambria and is proceeding towards us; but that is no reason for you to delay your mission, my friend. If my information is correct, the Gwenfo may already be aware of my presence here. Since they will not be willing to give up their knowledge of the hidden gold, the tribe may be preparing to flee. That cannot be allowed to happen."

"Then my men will need to ready themselves for a speedy departure."

Sulla nodded with satisfaction. "I suggest we mobilise them at once."

Without further delay, Darius then accompanied Sulla out of the villa, leaving Valeria to contemplate the grim implications of all that she had heard. She now knew, without a doubt, that her friends at the Dinas would soon be in very grave peril indeed, not so much from Darius – whom Valeria considered a fair-minded man – but from the commander who would follow him: Diophantus.

It had occurred to Valeria that she might try appealing to Darius once more for assistance; but, from what had been said moments before, Darius appeared to have convinced himself that his superiors wished him to obey Sulla's commands. Besides, it now seemed unlikely that anyone in the fort could have a conversation with the Tribune without Sulla being aware of the fact.

In all her endeavours, Valeria had never been one to be easily daunted; but at no time since Sulla's arrival had the girl felt so powerless to influence the course of events as she now did. For a fleeting moment, she found herself thinking of Rhidian and of his openness to the possibility of believing in the God of the Gwenfo tribe. If only, thought the girl, such a god could thwart the likes of Sulla, then he would be a god worth worshipping.

By this point, Valeria had emerged from her hiding place behind the chest and was standing beside the table where Darius and Sulla had been seated just moments before. The remains of their meal were plainly to be seen, but there was also something else: a small document. The girl realised that it must be the order from Baronius – the one which had so influenced Darius in his decision to do Sulla's bidding. Casting her eye down the parchment, Valeria happened to notice a few words, all on their own, beneath the main message: *"dispatch by means of carrier pigeon."*

In itself, it was no great surprise to learn that Sulla and his friends might be using carrier pigeons to send messages to each other, for the practice was common enough in Cambria. With the co-operation of the legionaries travelling from fort to fort, a regular exchange of pigeons was always taking place so that the appropriate birds would be ready to fly at a moment's notice.

Valeria was about to toss the document in her hand aside when a thought struck her. She remembered that the very fort she was in had a special building for birds, known as the aviary. It had suddenly occurred to the girl that if Sulla could communicate with his friends by means of pigeons, then why shouldn't she, Valeria, do the same with her friends?

There was just one person she knew of who would have the right to overrule Baronius's order and that was Constantius himself. If only the man could be persuaded to send a command stating that the local tribes should not be interfered with, then it might yet be possible for Valeria to turn Darius against Sulla.

From what Aaron and the others had reported, Valeria was aware that Constantius would be based, for the time being, some seventy miles from Luentinum at the fort of Isca Silurum. To make contact, it would therefore be essential for the girl to find a bird in the aviary which originated from the fort in question.

With this in mind, Valeria let herself out of the Prefect's Villa. She could see Sulla and his men at the far side of the compound, helping Darius to prepare for his departure. When satisfied that they were all fully distracted, Valeria picked her way by stealth towards the area of the fort where the aviary had been sited. It was at a location behind the barracks which, thankfully, were completely deserted.

The aviary was octagonal in shape with a low, pointed roof and a single doorway. On entering, Valeria was confronted by a far larger number of pigeons than she had anticipated, most of them in cage-like compartments with labels to indicate the origins of the birds. A few were from forts nearby, but most were from points much further afield. All the pigeons had been fitted with leg attachments – in the form of either metal rings or leather loops – to which messages could be fastened.

Valeria eventually spotted what she had been looking for: the birds from Isca Silurum. There were just two of them. All that was required now was a message for them to send. Valeria sat down at a desk that had been placed in the centre of the aviary. Upon it was a quill pen, some ink and various strips of parchment that, no doubt, had been left where they were for precisely the kind of purposes now in hand.

Valeria wrote a hurried message to Constantius imploring him to send any assistance he could and to issue an order to the effect that the tribes of the Towy Valley were to be left in peace. The girl copied the same message onto a second parchment. She then rolled up both parchments and took them over to where the pigeons were kept.

With great care, Valeria removed each of the Isca Silurum pigeons from their compartments and fastened the messages to them with the assistance of the leg attachments already in place. A number of small carrying cages were strewn around the floor of the aviary; these Valeria now used to restrain the pigeons for the moment when they would be ready for release outside. The girl placed one of the caged birds under the desk and then took the other to the open door of the aviary where the creature was allowed to escape.

To Valeria's consternation, however, the bird seemed in no hurry to embark on its journey. It fluttered around for a while before perching on the pointed roof of the aviary. Valeria picked up a few pebbles and attempted to dislodge the creature. Eventually, after much abuse from below, the bird extended its wings once more and took to the air – but not for long.

Within the space of a few short moments, events moved fast. Valeria heard the sound of an object whistling through the air and then, almost immediately, the pigeon overhead dropped to the ground, the shaft of an arrow protruding from its breast.

Valeria spun round to discover a triumphant-looking Sulla standing nearby with a bow in his hand. He strode across to the spot where the lifeless bird lay, prodded it with his feet and then examined the message attached to the leg.

"Your dove will fly no longer," gloated Sulla. "And neither, therefore, will the message which it bears."

The Decurio ordered his men to seize Valeria. She was marched into the aviary, where Sulla calmly examined the open bird cages and the tell-tale fresh ink markings near the quill pen. Valeria was desperately hoping that no-one would look underneath the desk, for the second pigeon would still be there, where it had been left, ready to fly at a moment's notice. If only the girl could have the opportunity of opening the cage . . .

"So," declared Sulla, seemingly satisfied with his inspection, "it appears that your attempt to hinder me has failed."

"Not for long," retorted Valeria, bitterly. "You won't get away with what you're doing here."

"Oh really? And what precisely is it about my actions that you find so distasteful?"

"Well, for one thing, just think about what you did to poor Rhidian, at the Mithras Temple."

Sulla's eyes narrowed. "I was not aware that you were acquainted with young Rhidian. How interesting. Perhaps you have a certain . . . fondness for the boy?"

"You wouldn't understand," said Valeria, uncomfortably. "But there was no need to set a bull on him. Why did you do it?"

"For a very simple reason – I wished to dissuade him from becoming a follower of the Way."

"From becoming a follower of the Way? But what would be so terrible about that? I mean, that bull of yours could have *killed* Rhidian."

"In the Eastern Empire, people are killed every day for far less serious crimes than for being followers of the Way. Besides, your friend survived his ordeal and, what is more, came through it courageously. In time, he will live to thank me; and then I look forward to having him join me in my battle against the people of the faith."

"Battle . . . against the people of the faith?" echoed Valeria, feeling astonished by what she had heard. The idea that Sulla might be more interested in hunting down followers of the Way than in searching for gold was a possibility that the girl had not seriously considered. She now realised that Aaron and the others had been right to suspect the Decurio of harbouring a concealed motive for his visit, for that indeed was what he now appeared to have.

Valeria's confusion had evidently been sensed by Sulla, for the man lost no time in exploiting it. "It seems," he noted with glee, "that like my noble new friend, Darius, you have allowed yourself to be misled by my title. Do not be fooled. I am no ordinary inspector of mines. My true work here concerns not gold, but something far more rare; some might even say – priceless. I refer to certain manuscripts that are known to be kept in the hideout of the Gwenfo tribe. No doubt, you are already familiar with the place and what it contains."

Valeria said not a word.

"Oh, come come, young lady. You know as well as I do that you have found refuge with the Gwenfo tribe this past few days. Do you really expect me to believe that, in that time, you were never introduced to the sacred manuscripts?"

"What if I was?" snapped the girl, defiantly.

"Then you must be aware that the ideas contained within them are seditious and pose a grave threat to the stability of the Empire."

"If you mean that the manuscripts teach followers of the Way that they must owe first allegiance to their god, rather than to Diocletian, then that sounds quite sensible to me. Who, in their right mind, would wish to serve Diocletian anyway?"

Sulla glowered. "You are too well versed in the language of disloyalty to Rome for your own good, as are many of your fellow islanders. It is small wonder that these shores have become a haven for followers of the Way. Those who administer this territory may call themselves Roman, but they do precious little to seize and destroy the copies of the sacred manuscripts which are used by the faithful to convert others to their beliefs."

"Why do you speak of *destroying* manuscripts? Doesn't that just make people, like me, more interested in what they contain? If you really wanted to put people off the faith, wouldn't it be better to try undermining the ideas that these followers of the Way believe in?"

"How? Pray enlighten me."

"Well, I suppose you could start by attacking the central belief held by these people: that their Saviour, known as the Son of God, rose from the dead after he was executed by us, the Romans. After all, it is a rather dramatic thing to believe."

"There were attempts to discredit the story you mention when it first arose, over two hundred years ago. One of my ancestors was at the forefront of those efforts. He, along with many others, searched high and low for the body of the man in question, but they never found it. Had they been able to do so, it would have been possible to disprove the claim that the body had been raised from the dead."

"Oh," said Valeria. "Even so, it must be possible to think of some other way of showing that there is no truth in what the followers of the Way believe."

Sulla gave Valeria a strange look. "How can you be so sure that what they believe is *not* the truth?"

"I don't see how it can be," replied Valeria, puzzled by Sulla's question. "After all, if you believed in the existence of the god worshipped by these people, you would surely want to become a follower of the Way yourself."

"Would I? Are you sure? Have you never heard mention of the devil – of the one who is said to oppose the God of whom we speak? For the followers of the Way have a saying: *'even the devil believes in God'*. If that be true, it would follow, would it not, that those who might consider themselves to be in league with the devil could believe in God while also opposing Him."

Valeria shuddered. "I don't understand. Are you saying that you think of *yourself* as being somehow . . ."

"In league with the devil? As to that question, unbeliever, it is for you to judge."

"But what about your ancestor – the one who searched for the body of the man said, by followers of the Way, to have been raised from the dead? After all

168

that searching, he must have come to some decision about whether the story was true or not."

"He did indeed; and, for better or worse, the legacy of his decision has reverberated down the generations of my kinsmen to the present day. I know not what dark experiences drove him to do so, but in a certain Mithras Temple north of Rome my ancestor swore under oath to oppose followers of the Way and, what is more, committed us, his descendants of the male line, to follow that example. So it was that I, upon reaching manhood, swore an oath in the same Temple of Mithras as did my father, and his father before that, to do all in my power to hunt down the people of the faith and destroy their manuscripts."

"Surely you cannot expect to slow down the spread of this faith by destroying manuscripts?"

"And why not? You have said yourself that it is by undermining the beliefs of these followers of the Way that their movement may be checked. What better way to accomplish that than by destroying the manuscripts in which those beliefs are laid down. For even when freely available, there are those within the communities of the faithful who doubt the plain meaning of the Scriptures; what delightful confusion might be caused, to the greater glory of the evil one, if the Scriptures were to disappear entirely!"

"But don't the writings say something to the effect that the words of the Lord will never pass away?"

Sulla looked uncomfortable for a moment; he soon

regained his composure, however. "Rest assured, young lady, that when the history of our time is recalled in the centuries to come, it will not be the followers of the Way, or their God, who are remembered most but, rather, the Emperor Diocletian. Why, the very years of our calendar are numbered from his reign. That is an honour which has yet to be bestowed upon the man who claimed to be the Son of God!"

Valeria had no time to respond, for at that moment the door of the aviary opened and a number of legionaries entered. It was just what the girl had been waiting for ever since her first carrier pigeon had been shot down by Sulla.

At the instant when those around her were distracted by the arrival of the legionaries, the girl grabbed her second pigeon, from its cage beneath the table, and made a dash for the door. Two of Sulla's men tried to head her off, but they only succeeded in colliding with each other, allowing Valeria to slide between them and out into the open air. Once there, the girl released her pigeon and, with it, all her hopes for a speedy response from Constantius.

It crossed Valeria's mind that had she been a follower of the Way, she would undoubtedly have prayed to her god at this point; she couldn't help but wonder whether such a god, if he existed, would ever be prepared to act in favour of a non-believer, like herself.

Valeria had little time to reflect on these matters, however, for Sulla and his men had soon caught up with the girl. They held her and watched in anger as the carrier pigeon cleared the battlements of the fort. As it did so, its rapidly receding form suddenly became bathed in an intense white glow. The effect lasted for a moment or two and then disappeared altogether – along with the bird.

After they had witnessed the phenomenon, Sulla's men began to mutter nervously among themselves.

"It is an ill omen for us," whispered one. "That bird was a dove and such creatures are a symbol of our enemies – the followers of the Way."

"Silence, fools!" thundered Sulla. "Have you never observed the effect of sunlight reflected off metal? You may depend upon it: that bird had a metal ring on its leg. How else could it convey its message?"

Sulla turned to Valeria and held her menacingly in his gaze. "Am I not right, young lady? You handled the bird. Was it not fitted with a ring?"

Now the truth was that Valeria could not remember whether there had been any metal rings on the legs of the pigeons she had used, for some of the birds in the aviary had been fitted with leather loops instead; but when the girl told Sulla of this, the Decurio was greatly angered.

"You know as well as I do," he fumed, "that the bird you released was ringed. No doubt you hope to undermine our confidence by attributing what was plainly an illusion of light to the hand of divine providence. I shall not fall for it."

171

"Your men did," said Valeria, slowly. "And perhaps they are right to be afraid. Maybe the legions of Constantius are, even now, bearing down upon this valley to destroy you all!"

"I think not," retorted Sulla, "for apart from those supporting me, there are no armies within sixty miles of here that are capable of posing a threat to us."

"You cannot be sure of that."

"Enough!" snapped Sulla. "We have no further time for these idle distractions. My men and I have a mission to accomplish; but before we proceed with it, there is one small matter which requires attention."

Sulla motioned his men to hold Valeria firmly.

"For your acts of treachery to Rome," continued the Decurio, "you will pay a heavy price – one which ensures that you are no longer in a position to stand in my way again."

CHAPTER TWELVE

# The Black Beast of Mallaen

From the overlook near the basket chasm, Rhidian and the others stared down with trepidation at the figures moving around the base of the Dinas. "We're outnumbered!" muttered Iago. "By a long way. The Romans have our West Door covered. We can't get out down the chasm any more – that much is certain."

"What about the North Door?" asked Eifiona, grimly. "Is the ladder entrance blocked?"

Iago nodded. "I checked that. Whoever is in charge of those legionaries knows exactly where to position his men for greatest effect."

Events were moving much faster than Rhidian would have liked. An escape from the Dinas now seemed out of the question. Not that any of the members of the Gwenfo tribe wished to leave, for they were all agreed on the vital importance of guarding the sacred manuscripts – the *deposit*, as they put it – until help should come from outside. For Rhidian, however, the arrival of the legionaries appeared to have destroyed the boy's chances of mounting the planned expedition to rescue his tribe. Neither, it seemed, would it now be possible for the boy to find Valeria and help her raise resistance to Sulla.

This, at least, was the way things appeared to be until Iago spoke up and reminded everyone of something they had almost forgotten about – the remains of Towser's flying craft. Was it not possible, the lamplighter wondered, that just such a craft – of which a number had been built – might be used to escape from the Dinas?

"Escape?" asked Eifiona, incredulously. "On a *cherub*? Who would wish to risk their neck in such a perilous enterprise?"

Iago shrugged. "Perhaps you're right. It was just a thought."

"I'll fly a *cherub*," said Rhidian, quickly. "There is no other way out of the Dinas. How else can I hope to reach my tribe at Dolaucothi?"

Eifiona gave the boy an affectionate squeeze on the shoulder. "We do not doubt your courage, Rhidian; but even if your flight were to prove a success, you surely could not hope to storm the gold mines without the help of others. No – I believe that it would be unwise of us to allow you to fly a *cherub* – but what does Aaron think?"

Rather to everyone's surprise, the pedlar shook his head in disagreement. "In my judgment, we oppose Rhidian's proposal at our peril; for the Lord is with

him. We must not forget the extraordinary circumstances in which the remains of the lost *cherub* were
discovered. Was it not Rhidian who, at the very moment
of his rebirth in the pool, became entangled in the submerged wreckage of Towser's invention? I am
convinced not only that we should allow the boy to fly
but that it is part of the Lord's plan that he does so."

There was an awkward pause while everyone considered the implications of what Aaron had said. It was
Eifiona who broke the silence.

"Well," she breathed, "let's see what the remaining
*cherubim* look like. Then, perhaps, we'll be in a better
position to judge whether or not it would be wise to use
one of them."

So it was that while Gwion and some of his friends
kept watch over the legionaries outside, Rhidian and
the others headed for the summit of the Dinas where
the remaining *cherubim* were known to have been
stored. According to Iago, Towser had chosen the
summit of the mountain as the launch site for all his
early experiments with flying craft. Since it seemed reasonable to hope that the higher the launch, the longer
the glide, Rhidian decided that he could probably do no
better than to follow in the footsteps of the airman who
had gone before him. At least, this was how the boy felt
until he was shown the exact spot that Towser had used
as his jumping-off point.

It was a fearsome spectacle. At the highest point of
the Dinas, out in the open air, was a smooth slab of

rock, angled steeply downwards. It had evidently been chosen to act as a kind of ramp for the would-be flyer to pick up speed before taking to the air; for at the end of the slab was a precipitous drop straight down to the valley floor with nothing but the occasional bushy outcrop to arrest the fall of any creature unfortunate enough, or foolhardy enough, to venture too close to the edge. Yet it was beyond this very edge that Rhidian was proposing to project himself. He stood ashen-faced while Iago proceeded to assemble the different parts of the *cherub* at the safe end of the slab of rock.

"I don't like it," murmured Eifiona. "Even if Rhidian is able to fly well clear of the Dinas, there is no telling what difficulties the boy might then face. The Romans might well be capable of tracking the path of the *cherub* to the point where it reaches the ground; and when it does, Rhidian will still have to make his way to Dolaucothi on foot, and in broad daylight, with who knows how many legionaries prowling along the valley trails."

"You speak truly," replied Aaron. "Therefore, when Rhidian lands the *cherub*, he must avoid the valley trails and head for the mountain wastes of Mallaen."

"Mallaen?" inquired Eifiona, aghast. "Why must the boy go there?"

"Why? Because it is the one place that will be free of legionaries."

"Indeed it will; but there is good reason why that should be so; for Mallaen is a wilderness of grim repute that echoes only to the wail of the stalking beasts and other accursed disturbances that are a legacy from the pagan rituals of long ago . . ."

Eifiona broke off abruptly on noticing Rhidian's concerned expression. The Chief Scribe thought for a moment. She then produced an object that had been slung over her shoulder and showed it to the boy.

"See this?" she said. "It is the horn of a ram – a musical instrument of sorts. If you must leave us, it is my wish that you take this horn. I have found it invaluable on a number of occasions as a means of deterring dangerous beasts in the woods, or as a way of calling for help when alone in the wilderness.

"We are told in the Scriptures that the ancient Hebrews used trumpets made of rams' horns in their campaign against the city of a certain enemy. On the seventh day of the campaign, in accordance with God's commands, the Hebrews and their priests marched seven times around the enemy city, sounding their horns all the while. At the seventh turn, when they had done all that they had been instructed to do, the walls of the city came tumbling down – just as God had promised."

"But there are no cities in these parts," observed Iago, puzzled.

"True enough," replied Eifiona. "Nevertheless, there are enemies, are there not? Was it not one of the prophets of old who was appointed by God to be a watchman for his people; and was he not told, in effect, to sound his trumpet in the event of approaching danger? Therefore, I urge Rhidian to carry the ram's horn trumpet with him on his journey."

With Aaron nodding his approval, Rhidian took the horn and fastened it to his belt. As he did so, his hand brushed against the lodestone compass hanging around his neck.

"You will need that too," said the pedlar, pointing at the compass. "When you reach the top of the mountain of Mallaen, look for a certain crooked thorn tree – there is only one such tree on the part of the mountain that overlooks the valley. On reaching the crooked thorn, take your compass and use it so as to proceed due north-west. Stray neither to the left nor the right of that course, or else you may never escape the clutches of Mallaen.

"How, you may ask, can you be certain that you will be maintaining the correct heading for Dolaucothi? The answer is this: at the highest point of your journey, you will come upon the remains of an old tomb together with a certain ancient standing stone, its runed surface a testament to the vile incantations that were once uttered in its presence.

"Be wary of this diabolical object and keep your wits about you; for those who become followers of the Way must expect to be tested. Therefore, as is written in the Scriptures: *"Put on the whole armour of God that you may be able to stand against the wiles of the devil."*

By this point, Rhidian had started to wonder

whether he ought to forget about the entire expedition. It had begun to seem so much more complicated than he had first anticipated. However, Iago had just finished assembling the *cherub*. It was therefore too late for Rhidian to back out without appearing timid.

The flying craft was essentially constructed of wood with the exception of the tail and wing sections which were covered with a papyrus-like material. The entire frame was mounted on wheels for ease of movement along the ground. There was also a seat from which the person flying the *cherub* could control with his hands the positioning of the wings, and with his feet the alignment of the tail.

Rhidian clambered into the seat of the craft and spent some time experimenting with the controls before announcing that he was ready to proceed.

Aaron closed his eyes and began muttering something to himself. Iago gave Rhidian a reassuring pat on the back and then helped him into position at the top of the angled slab of rock.

"Once you're in the air," said the lamplighter, "ride with the flow of the wind if you can. Towser told me that the buzzards do it. It seems that there is a certain westerly air current, in particular, which is funnelled through the natural bottleneck at the head of this valley. If you can find the current, it should carry you well on your way to Mallaen."

"Godspeed – until next we meet," added Eifiona, her voice heavy with emotion.

By this point, Aaron had opened his eyes. He spoke with great solemnity. "Have no fear, young Rhidian. You will survive – it has been made known to me."

Rhidian gulped. Somehow, on this occasion, the pedlar's words seemed less reassuring than the boy would have liked.

After a final signal from Rhidian, Iago released the tail end of the *cherub* allowing it to move at ever-increasing speed towards the edge of the summit. An instant later, the craft shot over the precipice and took a sickening lurch towards the ground. It was as much as the horrified Rhidian could do to keep his grip on the frame of the *cherub*, let alone brake its fall; but then, almost as rapidly as it had begun, the stomach-wrenching sensation passed and the dive began to level out into a glide, of sorts. Nevertheless, these were terrifying moments for the boy as he struggled to work out how to handle his craft.

Out of the corner of his eye, Rhidian noticed the rocky prominence of the Dinas gradually receding behind him. Down below, the Romans had evidently noticed that something strange was afoot, for some of them appeared to be staring upwards in the boy's direction. A number of the legionaries began to run along the ground with the apparent intention of pursuing the object above them. However, they soon disappeared from view and Rhidian was left to the all-important task of manoeuvring his craft onto the right course.

Already, the boy was beginning to feel the phenomenon that Iago had spoken of – the pulling effect of the westerly current of air that funnelled itself through the bottleneck of the valley below the Dinas and beyond. It was this current of air which now threatened to drag the *cherub* dangerously close to the ridges of the valley to Rhidian's right. In an attempt to correct this, the boy leaned over to his left and adjusted the tail fin with his feet. To his relief, the craft responded immediately and, before long, it was back on the right course with the sides of the river valley at a safe distance on either side and the slopes of the mountain of Mallaen looming up ahead.

Rhidian could scarcely believe that he was truly airborne. Had it not been the dream of men from the earliest times to fly like a bird? Yet here was Rhidian, defying even the might of the Roman army from the untouchable heights. The boy could not savour such sentiments for long, however, for he soon became aware that the *cherub* was showing signs of a decrease in forward motion combined with an increase in the rate of descent. These facts, Rhidian concluded, could be explained by the sudden absence of the westerly air current that had so assisted the first part of the flight. Now that he was descending more rapidly, the question of how best to manage a landing came to the fore of the boy's mind.

The mountain of Mallaen now filled the horizon and it became apparent that the *cherub* would strike the slopes at a lower level than Rhidian had earlier thought. The boy carefully moved himself into a position where, if necessary, he would be able to jump out of the *cherub* at a moment's notice. Already, Rhidian was being buffeted by a powerful new current of air sweeping down the Llyfnant Valley to the right and it was all the boy could do to prevent the craft from being overturned.

An expanse of grass on the lower slopes of the mountain ahead appeared to offer the best chance of a soft landing. Yet although Rhidian attempted to guide the *cherub* towards the grass, it soon became clear that the boy would fly beyond the area in question by a wide margin. Indeed, by the looks of things, he was about to crash into a ravine.

With just moments to spare before impact, Rhidian leapt out of the *cherub* and dived into what looked like a soft area of grass. Unfortunately, the boy struck the ground awkwardly and began to roll back down the slope. It was only when he slid into a patch of rocks that Rhidian's body finally came to rest, his head striking an object in the process. As he slipped into unconsciousness, the boy was dimly aware of the final moments of the *cherub*, splintering and tearing its way to the bottom of the ravine.

One of the first things Rhidian noticed when he finally opened his eyes was how dark his surroundings had become. It was not immediately clear whether this was due to a considerable lapse of time since the crash of the *cherub*, or simply to a rapid change in the weather. In any event, the temperature had certainly dropped.

Rhidian slowly picked himself up, nursing a bruise to his head. While gathering his strength, he peered over the edge of the nearby ravine. There it was: Towser's proud achievement, stretched across a mountain brook, its wings in shreds and its tail section twisted around an old tree stump. That this *cherub* would never fly again was plain to see. Rhidian vowed to himself that if he ever had the opportunity, he would try to build a replacement. For the time being, there was some comfort in the knowledge that at least the Romans would be unlikely to find the remains of the *cherub* where it had ended up; and even if anyone did find the craft, it would certainly be of no use to them.

Rhidian turned to face the slopes of Mallaen. He decided that if he was to reach the top quickly, he could do no better than to follow the ravine upwards until he reached the source of the brook that flowed within. It would be a steep ascent; that much was clear. Rhidian had scarcely taken more than a few paces when he felt a faint, cold sensation on the back of his hand. He soon saw the explanation: it had begun to snow. Aaron had evidently been right to suspect a possible change in the weather. All the more reason, thought the boy, to press on with the journey before conditions worsened.

At first, the ascent was eased by the presence of the many sheep trails that criss-crossed the ravine; but the higher he went, the more Rhidian was forced to proceed

on all-fours, pulling himself up with the help of convenient rocks and clumps of heather. The soil, such as
it was, had begun to feel damp and slippery, making
progress all the more difficult. When he reached the
crags high up the slope, beneath what appeared to be
the top of the mountain, Rhidian looked back over his
shoulder. The sight of the sheer drop below was more
than enough to convince him that retreat was now out
of the question. The boy therefore continued to inch his
way upwards, clambering from one rock to another. It
was a strenuous task and by the time he had finally
hauled himself to safety above the crags, Rhidian was
suffering from yet more bruising to his already sore
limbs.

The ridge on which the boy now found himself was
already covered with a layer of snow, the result of the
flakes that had been falling steadily for some time; but
if the state of the weather was unfortunate, an even
greater concern was the way in which the sky seemed
to be turning ever darker. Rhidian had to face the fact
that this was probably due to the lateness of the hour
and that a considerable period of time must have
elapsed between the crash of the *cherub* and the boy's
waking. Still, there was nothing that could be done
about this most unwelcome development.

As he lay recovering from his climb, Rhidian spotted
the landmark that he had been warned to look out for:
the crooked thorn. Its contorted appearance seemed
almost inevitable in view of the windswept location

where it grew. The boy picked himself up and tramped the hundred paces or so that it took to reach the tree.

Rhidian pulled out the lodestone compass that Aaron had given him and held it in such a way that the direction of the arrow filament and the symbol for *North* were in alignment. The boy was well aware, however, that this initial adjustment was just the easy part of the task ahead. The real difficulty lay, while walking, in maintaining the setting of the lodestone and thereby travelling in a straight line north-west to Dolaucothi. Just how successfully this could be done – in failing light, and in an atmosphere thick with snow – was something that had yet to be discovered.

As Rhidian left the crooked thorn behind him, he could not avoid being struck by the loneliness of the expanse over which he was embarking. It was a scene in transformation – a landscape of barren knolls and heather-lined hollows, all steadily being buried beneath the snow. Indeed, the wind was picking up and beginning to cause blizzard-like conditions, making the boy's progress increasingly difficult. Eventually, after what seemed like miles, Rhidian caught sight of something in the distance. It was a dark, pointed object, its shape at first only just visible through the driving snow; but gradually, as its form became clearer, Rhidian realised what was looming up ahead – it was the ancient standing stone about which Aaron had so fervently warned.

A little to the south of the stone was a prominent mound. It seemed certain that this must be the old tomb that had earlier been mentioned by the pedlar. Rhidian had no particular wish to see either the stone or the tomb at close quarters; but if he was to remain on the course indicated by the compass, as he had been told to do, then past both stone and tomb he would have to go.

Before long, the boy was able to make out the features of these landmarks more clearly. For one thing, he noticed that the tomb in fact consisted of a pile of boulders with a small door sunk into the side. As for the ancient stone, stark against the skyline, its dark, leaning form mesmerised Rhidian. He had the strangest feeling that he had seen it somewhere before – in the distant past.

As he approached, he couldn't help but notice that the object was marked, just as Aaron had said it would be, with certain strange symbols; but what particularly caught the boy's eye was a flash of colour near the base. Taking care not to touch anything, Rhidian warily moved in for a closer look at the stone. Painted onto the surface, in pigments of various shades, was a depiction of a chilling scene.

On one side was what looked like a small crowd of people. One man, in particular, had a knife, or dagger, in his hand. Much to Rhidian's disquiet, the man appeared to be in the process of throwing his weapon at another person who was restrained by thick ropes. The figure of this second person was small enough to be that of a child. Whoever the victim might be, he or she clearly had little chance of survival; for, apart from the dagger, a further threat to life appeared to come from something else in the scene – a large, black, four-legged beast, its teeth bared for attack.

The implication of these images was clear: that after being struck by the dagger, the victim would then be devoured by the fearsome-looking creature nearby. Given the history of Mallaen as a site of pagan worship, it seemed all too likely that the picture was a representation of a sacrifice that had taken place on the mountain at some point in the past. The question was: when might such a sacrifice have taken place?

The fact that the images had been *painted*, rather than having been etched or carved, provided a possible clue. In the damp, windswept climate of the Cambrian mountains, most of the coloured pigments that Rhidian had come across usually weathered away within a few years of being exposed to the elements. The boy knew this from what had remained of his own early attempts at rock painting.

Yet if a sacrifice had indeed taken place on the mountain only a few years before, who had been responsible for it? Rhidian didn't have to look far to find the answer. Concealed beneath the picture on the stone was a small, painted design. With a shock, the boy realised that he was staring at something very familiar – the sign of the black crow. It was the distinctive emblem of Rhidian's tribe. In a flash, the boy understood what the presence of the sign probably meant: that the Ewenni tribe had somehow been involved in the sacrifice, perhaps even to the extent that one of their number had been the man with the dagger. Then more thoughts began to crowd in on Rhidian. Who exactly were the other figures in the picture meant to represent? Were they all supposed to be members of the Ewenni tribe? And why was it that Rhidian himself had felt such an uncanny familiarity with the ancient stone, despite the fact that he had never knowingly visited it before? Was it possible that the boy, when he had been too young to memorise it properly, had been taken up the mountain and been made an unwitting party to a sacrifice?

If so, it accounted for a great deal. It would have explained the fact that Rhidian, for as long as he could recall, had always harboured a strange fear of climbing Mallaen. It would have explained also, perhaps, why Aaron had felt driven to call the Ewenni people to repentance; for it seemed that their hands might be drenched with the blood of an innocent child.

There remained the question: to what extent were Aaron, and the members of the tribe, aware of these matters? It was a question that could wait, Rhidian decided; for the snow was becoming heavier by the moment and the boy knew that he ought to find some shelter before the light faded completely. Unfortunately, there appeared to be no shelter in sight, with the possible exception of the old tomb; and that was hardly more appealing as a place of refuge than the standing stone itself.

Rhidian was about to begin searching for something further afield when he heard a piercing sound from over his shoulder. It was an unearthly, long-drawn-out wail of a kind that would have chilled the vitals of the bravest of warriors. Rhidian dared not look round. Instead, he began to run for the tomb as fast as he could; and well he might, for he could now hear behind him the footfalls of a heavy creature bounding through the snow.

The distance Rhidian had to cover was greater than he had first thought, but at last he reached the tomb and flung open the wooden door at the entrance. Out of the corner of his eye, the boy caught sight of a dark shape hurtling towards him. There was not a moment to lose. No sooner had Rhidian shut himself into the tomb than he heard the impact of what he assumed was the creature crashing headlong into the wooden door that now blocked its path.

An eerie silence followed, but then came the sound of heavy paws shuffling stealthily over the rocks and boulders that covered the roof of the enclosure. Was there another way into this place? Rhidian fervently hoped not. He sank to the ground, breathing heavily and yet remaining fully alert. After a time, it became clear that the creature, whatever it was, had failed to penetrate the tomb. The sound of feet among the boulders overhead gradually subsided and then stopped altogether. Gingerly, Rhidian edged the door of the tomb open a fraction until he could see what lay outside. Unfortunately, the creature was still there, its dark shadow moving slowly to and fro against the snow.

The boy decided that he could do little else but remain within the tomb until the stalker outside departed. The matter of when that might be was uncertain. Perhaps it would even be necessary to wait until morning. The thought of staying the night in the dark, musty atmosphere of the tomb filled the boy with dread; but he was at least able to content himself with the knowledge that to try any other plan at that moment would be folly.

Rhidian did his best not to think of the many skeletons that undoubtedly lay in the darkness just feet away from him. He sat as near to the door of the tomb as possible, drew himself into a ball-like shape and pulled his cloak over his knees for extra warmth. Then, with the muffled sounds of the blizzard raging outside, Rhidian gradually drifted uneasily off to sleep – so uneasily, in fact, that his slumbers were soon plagued by strange dreams.

He had a vision of a Roman official, accompanied by a number of legionaries, walking up to what looked like the entrance of a large cave with iron bars across the front. Behind the bars could be seen many people, some of whom were recognisable as slaves. The Roman official suddenly drew out a short sword, or knife, and began to pace to and fro, apparently talking to the people imprisoned in the cave. One of the men behind the bars then put out his hand and was given the sword to hold. He sliced the air with it a couple of times as if to test its handling qualities. As a result of this, or so it seemed, the man was let out of the cave by one of the nearby legionaries and was then directed to follow the Roman official along a path through some adjacent woods.

Still fast asleep, the boy soon found himself transported into another scene, this time within the confines of what looked like a Roman fortification of some kind. A number of the people from the previous scene were visible, but there was also another figure present, having the appearance of a child or young person. Rhidian was unable to make out the face, but he could see that this individual must be in some kind of danger, for he or she had been bound securely to a wooden post. A short distance away, the man who had been released from the cave in the earlier scene stood with a sword in his hand – undoubtedly the very same one he had handled before. To Rhidian's horror, he appeared to be preparing to throw it in the direction of the person tied to the post. It seemed that the sword was about to claim a victim; and as if that wasn't enough, something else had suddenly appeared on the scene – a ferocious-looking black beast, creeping relentlessly towards the trussed-up figure at the post.

Rhidian felt desperately that he ought to intervene in the events that he was witnessing. As if in answer to this call, the boy abruptly found himself face to face with the black beast, its teeth bared and its eyes seething with malice. Rhidian reached for his sword but could find only the ram's horn that Eifiona had given him. Instinctively, the boy placed the trumpet to his lips and blew on it – once. The creature recoiled immediately. Slowly, but deliberately, and sounding the ram's horn as he went, Rhidian began to circle round his cowering adversary – again and again. By the time he had completed a seventh turn, the boy had become dizzy. His surroundings began to look blurred, he felt himself drop to the ground, and he awoke from his dream with a start.

Rhidian opened his eyes to the sensation of bright sunshine on his face. His first thought was one of relief that the images of the dream still imprinted on his mind had no connection with reality; but this sentiment soon passed when it became clear to the boy that although he still appeared to be positioned on the mountain of Mallaen, he was no longer located in the tomb – the place where he had laid his head the night before. In fact, much to his consternation, Rhidian found that he was now lying with his head against the ancient standing stone. It was a circumstance that seemed to defy explanation. The boy had no recollection of having walked between the tomb and the stone and neither had he any memory of being carried that distance by some other means.

Rhidian rose to his feet and studied his surroundings. Although the skies had now cleared, the territory round about was still thick with snow and it was this fact that provided the boy with the clue as to how he had come to be in his present position. There, clearly visible upon the white landscape were some footprints, the same size as Rhidian's, leading to the ancient stone from the direction of the tomb. Was it possible that Rhidian might somehow have walked through the snow in his sleep? The boy could think of no other explanation as to how he could have moved across the gap between the tomb and the stone.

Rhidian began to examine the footprints in the snow more carefully. He noticed that they passed right round the ancient stone – not just once, but *seven* times in all. Indeed, it was the very fact that there were *seven* such circles of footprints that intrigued the boy most of all; for was that not also the number of times Rhidian had circled around the black beast in his dreams? And where black beasts were concerned, what of the *real* one that had emerged from the wilderness the night before? Where had it gone?

Rhidian cast his eyes to the ground once more in search of clues. Sure enough, he soon found another set of tracks, this time undoubtedly belonging to a large animal. These prints, like the human ones, came from the direction of the tomb. The boy followed the tracks to the far side of the ancient stone. Here he made a startling discovery: on the ground lay Rhidian's own sword, covered with blood. In the surrounding snow, too, there were tell-tale patches of crimson. These led off across the mountain for as far as the eye could see.

The creature had evidently been struck by Rhidian's sword and was now somewhere out there in the wilderness – injured.

Though he was aware that such an animal could still be dangerous, the boy felt greatly relieved by what he had seen. Somehow, he knew that in wounding the black beast, no matter how superficially, a battle of a kind had been won, not merely of flesh and blood, but also in the spiritual realm. That the creature was a manifestation of the devil, Rhidian had little doubt. After all, Aaron had spoken of the existence of just such an unearthly animal.

Yet if the beast had been put to flight, what did it mean for Rhidian? Was it a sign that the boy's spiritual battle was in some sense already won? Or simply a sign that in all such battles, the invisible hand of the Lord would always be at work? Either way, these questions could not be separated from the mystery of Rhidian's dream; for within it had appeared a cat-like animal similar to the *real* beast of Mallaen. Perhaps, therefore, just as the creature in the dream had a connection with one in real life, the incidents in the dream might similarly have a connection with real-life events. The problem was: what might those events be?

Rhidian glanced at the ancient stone with its painting now much more clearly visible than it had been the night before. It was then that it came home to the boy how similar were the visions he had experienced in his dream to the images on the stone. In both cases, the theme was of an attempted sacrifice, or killing, where the perpetrator was a man wielding a blade, of some kind, and the victim a child or young person. Also in both cases, the immediate danger to the victim was compounded by the presence of a black beast poised for attack.

To Rhidian's mind, the unpleasantness of a possible knife-wound paled into insignificance next to that of being devoured by a wild animal. Besides, this particular animal clearly represented much more than merely a threat to the body. It endangered soul and spirit also. If the person in Rhidian's dream existed, it was therefore vital that he or she should be warned of the peril before it was too late. The situation reminded the boy of the words Eifiona had uttered on handing him the ram's horn trumpet: "*Was it not one of the prophets of old who was appointed by God to be a watchman for his people; and was he not told, in effect, to sound his trumpet in the event of approaching danger?*" It was all very well, thought Rhidian; but how was it possible to sound a trumpet and warn the victim represented in the dream if the identity of that person was unknown?

An unpleasant thought then crossed the boy's mind: what if the dream had been a warning concerning Valeria and that an attempt was about to made on her life? It was something that didn't bear thinking about. Yet the more he considered the matter, the more Rhidian became convinced that the possibility he had envisaged was real. Indeed, it was all too plausible.

After all, in the dream, had there not been a Roman fort in which a certain prisoner was to be executed? And had Valeria not been on a mission that would have taken her close to such a fort – Luentinum? As for Luentinum, was that not also where the gold mines were located and where groups of slaves would be kept – in particular, those pressed into service from the Ewenni tribe? And in the dream, had it not been a slave who had been chosen to dispatch the prisoner in the fort? Many of the facts, as Rhidian believed them to be, appeared to tally only too well with the visions he had experienced – all of them pointing to the urgency of the task before him.

Rhidian consulted his compass and, turning his back on the ancient stone, began walking as fast as he could in the direction of Dolaucothi.

CHAPTER THIRTEEN

# The Return of the Dove

Although the territory remained uneven, Rhidian forged ahead across the mountain as if travelling along a Roman road, neither straying from his course nor relenting his pace. In this, he was assisted both by the downward slope of the land and by the thinning out of the snow on the lower levels. As the boy advanced, patches of greenery began to appear, accompanied by the sound of early meltwaters flowing into the stream-beds round about.

The first indication of a Roman presence on the mountain came soon enough in the form of a water channel, or duct, cut into the soil. This, no doubt, was connected with the mines, for it led off in the direction of Dolaucothi. Rhidian followed the duct downwards for about a quarter of a mile. As he did so, he noticed a rapid transformation in his surroundings. The overnight snow had evidently long since melted at these low levels, leaving a damp, grey landscape in place of the earlier white. Gone was the pristine wilderness of the mountain-top. In its place could be seen the contours of an altogether less natural expanse. Mounds of displaced rock lay all around together with the remains of old iron tools, broken-down carts and discarded pieces of rope. Rhidian had reached the mines – of that, there seemed little doubt.

That the place was a Roman establishment was confirmed, if any confirmation were needed, by the sudden appearance of a number of legionaries. They had emerged from what looked like the mouth of an underground tunnel. Fortunately, the men marched off almost as quickly as they had appeared; but they had provided Rhidian with an important clue as to where he might proceed next.

The boy scrambled across to the tunnel entrance and peered inside. From the many oil lamps strung along the roof of the passage, it seemed reasonable to suppose that this route into the mines had to be one of some importance. After making sure that the immediate way ahead was clear, Rhidian stepped into the tunnel and began to proceed underground. The passage had evidently been hewn through rock, the pick-axe marks along the walls bearing ample testimony to the many slaves who had undoubtedly been put to work at Dolaucothi over the years. It was to prevent his own tribe from being forever condemned to such a fate that Rhidian now pressed ahead with more determination than ever.

The boy had scarcely moved more than twenty paces,

however, when he began to hear voices from somewhere up ahead. He hesitated, wondering whether to back off or not; but, as the moments passed and the voices began to trail off, Rhidian felt emboldened to proceed. Creeping further along the tunnel, he eventually came up against an obstacle: the way ahead had been blocked off by a wall of bricks and mortar. In the centre of the wall was a bolted iron door. From the far side of it could be heard the voices Rhidian had first noticed moments earlier – voices that now sounded distinctly non-Roman in character. Was it possible that they belonged to members of the Ewenni tribe?

Fingers trembling with excitement, the boy drew back the bolts on the door and flung it open. Sure enough, there beyond the wall, in what amounted to a small cave, was Rhidian's tribe – or what remained of it, for their number seemed less than the boy remembered it to have been. Looking pale and drawn, the occupants of the cave were huddled together beneath the only object of comfort available to them – a flickering oil lamp.

Rhidian's arrival was greeted with an astonished silence. In the dim light of the cave, no-one seemed able to recognise him at first. It was the boy's parents, Elgan and Gwawr, who finally realised the truth; and when they did, they became jubilant beyond measure, despite the presence of shackles on their wrists and ankles. Indeed, these very shackles almost caused Rhidian an injury, such was the enthusiasm of the embrace his parents gave him. It was a powerfully emotional moment for the boy, too, so relieved was he to find his family unharmed. Nor was the significance of the occasion lost on the rest of the tribe. They almost fell over themselves in an effort to welcome the new arrival in the cave. It was Rhidian who had to calm everyone down and remind them of what would now need to be done in order finally to escape from the mines.

First, there was the problem of how to rid people of their chains. The most effective means of accomplishing this, someone suggested, would be to use iron tools of the kind the Romans allowed slaves to carry in the mines. Such tools, it seemed, were handed out during supervised digging operations and, afterwards, were taken back and placed in a storage area until needed again.

Following the directions he was given, Rhidian ran off to find the tool store in question. From the large quantity of implements that he found there, he took a selection of hammers and chisels. These he carried back to the tribe and set to work breaking shackles – his parents' first. It was a laborious task, but once Elgan and Gwawr were free, they were able to take chisels of their own and help break the chains of other people in the cave. Soon, the tribe was in a position to post sentries at the mouth of the tunnel to watch out for any approaching Romans. The precaution enabled those who remained underground to continue breaking chains more single-mindedly than would otherwise have been possible.

Once the last person had been set free, no-one needed any prompting as to where the tribe should head next – almost anywhere except the mines, it seemed. Indeed, many were already waiting nervously under some trees in the open air for their fellow tribesfolk to emerge above ground. The whole company was about to move off when Rhidian noticed that someone particularly significant was missing from their number.

"Where is Brân?" asked the boy.

"Do not concern yourself with *him*," replied Elgan. "Brân is no longer one of us. He is a traitor."

"A traitor?"

Elgan nodded gravely. "It all started yesterday when a couple of legionaries came back from the Cothi Dam carrying some strange-looking boxes that they had found. The curious thing was that Brân seemed to know something about the boxes. He told Sulla that he would demonstrate what they were for if only he could be released from the mines."

"These boxes," said Rhidian, slowly, "were they painted red on top?"

"Indeed they were."

"And did Brân explain their purpose?"

"All he said at first was that, if used properly, a single box could do the work of many legionaries. Naturally, Sulla was curious. He agreed to release Brân from the mines so that he could demonstrate what he knew . . ."

Rhidian was beginning to feel weak at the knees. From what his father had told him, it had become clear that what the Romans had discovered at the Dam had to have been the barrels of Cambrian Powder that the boy had left there on his fateful expedition over the Beddau Pass two nights earlier. If this was so, the Decurio now had in his hands a new power to do great harm. Aaron had been proved right again. After all, it had been he who had warned Rhidian not to take the Cambrian Powder out of the Dinas. Now the wisdom of the pedlar's advice, and the boy's foolishness in rejecting it, had become plain; for what mischief Sulla could cause with the knowledge of Cambrian Fire at his disposal was anyone's guess.

The boy's troubled state must have been evident to those around him, for everyone was staring intently in his direction.

"Is anything the matter, Rhidian?" asked Elgan, finally.

"There may be," admitted the boy. "It depends on how much Sulla knows about those boxes."

Elgan frowned. "Among the last things we heard was that Brân's attempt to use the boxes failed – something to do with the powder inside them being damp, I believe. Sulla became rather angry about it, but he did offer Brân one last chance to prove himself – a special test that the Decurio himself thought up.

"And that was our difficulty. You see, Brân wanted us all to help him carry out Sulla's test: something to do with causing a *firestorm* – whatever that means. We weren't worried about causing a *firestorm*, though. It

202

was what they proposed to do with it that shocked us. Brân had been asked by Sulla to test the boxes by using them as a weapon against a real person."

"Real person?" inquired Rhidian, alarmed.

Elgan nodded. "It seems that this particular individual has made an enemy of Sulla, but that neither he nor his men wish to take the action they consider necessary. They would rather someone else did it for them. No doubt, it's not every day that they decide to kill a young girl – and a Roman one at that."

At this last comment, Rhidian gasped. An appalling thought had suddenly occurred to him. It seemed all too probable that the girl whose life was in danger was none other than Valeria! After all, it was she who had set out the previous morning in the direction of Dolaucothi; and which other girl in so small an area could be described as an enemy of Sulla?

"I'll have to go back," declared Rhidian, at once. "The rest of you can carry on without me."

Elgan shook his head, sadly. "If you're hoping to help that girl, you'd better think again. She's being kept in the fort."

"Then that's where I'll have to go."

Elgan sighed. "We understand your sympathy for this girl, but . . ."

"I don't think you do."

"But don't you realise what you're up against? To breach the defences of a Roman fort would be almost impossible."

"Perhaps I could disguise myself as a Roman and get in that way."

"In order to do that, it would be necessary to steal an outfit from one of the legionaries; but since there are few Romans of your size around here, you'd better rule out that plan."

"Wait," said one of the Ewenni. "What about the sewer tunnel – the one that leads under the walls of the fort? It might be possible to enter secretly that way."

"It would be far too narrow," observed Elgan.

"For a fully-grown person, maybe," replied the other, "but not for a youngster."

"I'd better give it a try," said Rhidian, "unless anyone can think of a better idea."

Elgan looked uncomfortable. "I don't like it; but if you feel you must press ahead with the plan, we will help you as far as we can."

It was decided that the women and children of the Ewenni tribe would wait at a safe distance from Dolaucothi. The men, on the other hand, would accompany Rhidian as far as the sewer tunnel and then stay there, keeping a close eye on the fort in case they might be needed by the boy later.

So it was that after collecting a number of weapons and a torch from the mines, Rhidian, and those who were following him, headed for the area surrounding the fort. On the way, any remaining doubts that the boy might have had concerning Valeria's whereabouts were quickly dispelled when he spotted Trojan, the stallion, tied to a tree in a patch of woodland. Elgan, and the others, concerned that the horse might attract unwanted attention, led the creature to a nearby thicket where it would be better hidden from the prying eyes of the Romans.

The sewer tunnel, as Rhidian soon discovered, emerged in the woods just north of the fort. It was indeed narrow but, even so, there was one particularly useful feature – a ledge, running along the length of the tunnel for as far as the eye could see. The boy hoped that this would enable him to crawl along underground without having to use the channel carrying the waste from the fort.

With the others of his tribe anxiously looking on, Rhidian squeezed into the tunnel and began to work his way underground. At first, the main difficulty for the boy lay in heaving himself forwards with one hand while carrying his torch in the other. It was a skill he found himself unable to perfect and frequently he became tired and had to take rests so as to relieve his aching arm muscles. Eventually, a faint glow became visible from somewhere up ahead. Rhidian crawled eagerly towards it, anxious to ensure that his unpleasant journey through the dark should come to an end. With that thought uppermost, it came as a relief to find that at the end of the tunnel there were no doors or iron grills to be broken down. Rhidian was simply able to climb out into what looked like the basement of a bathhouse, or similar building, such was the extent of the piping running through it. Ascending a flight of stone steps, the boy found himself staring out into a compound bristling with hundreds of legionaries. That they were in the service of Sulla, there seemed little doubt, for some of them carried the Decurio's banner – the emblem of the white bull. But how had Sulla managed to raise such an army so quickly? Certainly, they had not been available to him at the time of his raid on the Ewenni camp.

Rhidian had little time to consider these matters, however, for he suddenly noticed something taking place on the far side of the fort. It was the scene he had been dreading: Valeria being paraded across the compound by Sulla. Rhidian's heart sank. It seemed likely that he would have to move fast if he was to prevent any harm coming to his friend.

The boy crept around the perimeter walls of the fort, taking care to keep himself hidden, in an effort to get as close as possible to Valeria. However, she, along with Sulla, Brân, and some of the legionaries, eventually disappeared into a small wooden shed – one with a distinctive conical roof. Rhidian worked his way over to the shed and tip-toed round the back, looking for a window or peep-hole of some kind. He discovered a couple of loose planks in one wall and, having carefully removed them, found that he was able to crawl through, on all-fours, onto the other side. From within, the purpose of the shed was immediately apparent, for it was filled with dozens of caged birds. Striking though this was, Rhidian's attention was soon focused on what was happening just a few feet away from him.

Brân was busy fastening Valeria to a chair positioned on a small raised platform at the centre of the shed. Yet it was what lay beneath the platform that alarmed the boy most of all. There, less than a foot beneath Valeria's seat, was one of the objects that the boy had originally left at the Mithras Temple – it was a barrel of Cambrian Powder. Rhidian was only too well aware that if it ignited, his friend would have little chance of survival.

Standing just in front of Valeria was Sulla. That he had little sympathy for the girl's plight was evident from the taunting manner of his voice.

"If I am not very much mistaken, young lady," he rasped, "it seems that your friend, Rhidian, has been a little careless. After all, the barrel of powder on which you are seated belongs to him, does it not?"

"I don't know what you mean," retorted the girl.

Sulla shrugged. "If that is so, then you really are of no further use to me. Had you been able to tell us the ingredients of Rhidian's mysterious powder, then it might have been possible for us to release you. Not that it really matters – we can always extract an answer from Rhidian himself . . ."

"You'll never find him," said Valeria, her voice trembling. "He's safely hidden from the likes of you."

"Safely hidden, eh? If he is skulking in the Dinas, as I suspect, then he will be in our hands sooner than you think."

"Your attack against the Dinas will not succeed. Remember the dove that got away? By now, it will have reached Constantius with my message."

Sulla laughed. "I was wondering when you might mention the pigeon again. Allow me to show you something."

The Decurio walked over to the door of the shed and shouted to someone outside. One of the legionaries came running, handed Sulla a small, square object and then left. It soon became clear that the object in question was a cage containing a pigeon. Sulla removed the creature from the cage, tucked it firmly under his arm and began to stroke its neck.

"This bird," stated the Decurio, "arrived here yesterday. It came from Isca Silurum."

"Is it carrying anything?" asked Valeria, quickly.

Sulla reached underneath the bird and drew out a piece of parchment from a small leather loop attached to the leg of the creature.

"Ah! What's this?" declared the Decurio, with mock surprise. "A message from Constantius? I shan't read it out to you, though. That would be too unkind. You have come close to thwarting my plans, young lady – and yet you will never know how close!"

"Tell me what the message says!" shouted Valeria, straining at the ropes that held her in position.

Sulla ignored the demand. He folded the parchment and placed it back into the loop on the pigeon's leg. As he did so, the bird suddenly slipped from his grasp and began to fly around the shed. Brân was ordered to try and catch the creature but it soon became clear that he was not equal to the task. Eventually, Sulla lost his patience.

"Leave the bird," he growled. "It will have to take its chances in the experiment like all the other pigeons here . . ."

From his hiding place in the corner of the shed, Rhidian had been listening to everything that had been said. In particular, he had pricked up his ears on hearing about the pigeon and the message it was supposed to have carried from Constantius. As a result, when the bird eventually flew into the boy's corner, he was understandably eager to try and catch it. Unfortunately, as soon as he reached out his hand to grab the creature, it fluttered off into a different area of the shed – an area that was in full view of Sulla.

However, Rhidian soon forgot about the movements of the pigeon when he saw what was happening elsewhere. Brân was attempting to gag Valeria. He finally succeeded but not without furious resistance from the girl. Although Rhidian desperately wanted to intervene immediately, he knew that the right moment had yet to arrive; so he waited.

Sulla was now standing directly in front of Valeria, his arms folded. When he spoke to the girl, the air of finality in his voice was unmistakable.

"Unfortunately," said the Decurio, "the time has come for us to bid each other farewell. I regret having to leave you under such circumstances. Of course, had you been a boy, then, as with Rhidian, we might have invited you to become a servant of Mithras in this life. Sadly, women are not permitted in the Brotherhood. But do not be distressed. I have no doubt that when you pass from this world to the other side, you will have your audience with Mithras – or, should I say, with the being who lies behind the mask of Mithras!"

With that, Sulla turned round and strode out of the bird shed, signalling to Brân as he went. The tribal chieftain then struck together two pieces of flint, creating a spark which he applied to the candle on the barrel of Cambrian Powder. The flickering flame that followed told its own story – before much longer, the powder would ignite! It was a fact of which Brân himself seemed only too well aware, for he soon dropped the pieces of flint and ran for the door of the shed.

Rhidian knew that he had just moments to spare. As soon as Brân had gone, the boy leapt out of his hiding place, raced across to Valeria's position and snuffed out the flame above the powder barrel. He then immediately set to work at removing the bonds that held his friend in position. As secure as these bonds were, they proved no match for Rhidian's sword and were soon in pieces on the floor.

Although the first part of his task was done, the boy lost no time in tackling the next: to re-light the candle on the powder barrel with the pieces of flint Brân had left behind. This was of vital significance if the Decurio was to be fooled into thinking that Valeria had not been rescued. In fact, Rhidian became so pre-occupied with the lighting of the candle that he had no time to remove either the ropes that still restrained Valeria's wrists or the gag that prevented her from speaking. By the time the girl was finally able to communicate, Rhidian was already pushing her towards the hole in the wall of the shed.

"The pigeon!" she gasped. "We must have it."

"Too late," replied the boy. "The powder's about to blow!"

Rhidian was right. He had scarcely managed to get his friend out into the open air and behind the nearest safe building when he heard the sound of the explosion. Out of the corner of his eye, he saw the entire structure of the bird shed collapse. There were pigeons every-where. Some were strewn on the ground, dead; others had escaped unharmed and were, even now, circling in the air above the fort.

Standing nearby with some of his men, seemingly mesmerised by the results of the explosion, was Sulla. Fortunately for Rhidian and Valeria, the Decurio was evidently too distracted to have noticed the escape that had just taken place to one side of him. Indeed, so com-plete was the destruction of the shed that Sulla didn't even bother to look closely for what might have remained of Valeria's body. No doubt, he would have felt such an exercise to be unnecessary; for stretched out on the ground beside the rubble was the body of a quite unexpected victim – Brân. Whether the chieftain had been about to re-enter the shed at the moment of his misfortune was unclear to Rhidian; but whatever the circumstances had been, Sulla evidently had no intention of mourning his former assistant.

"Make ready to ride," he growled at the legionaries standing beside him.

"And the rest of the powder?" asked one of the men. "What should we do with it?"

"Nothing!" declared Sulla. "That powder is too unreliable, as Brân has discovered to his cost. I, for one, have no desire to blow myself up. No, the Gwenfo tribe will be defeated with our usual weaponry."

Without further delay, Sulla turned and crossed over to the far side of the fort compound where the hundreds of legionaries that comprised his army had assembled. He then mounted his horse and, shouting the order to depart, led his men out through the gates of the fort. Such was the length of the marching column that the sound of people, horses and wagons on the move filled the air long after the Decurio himself had departed.

As soon as everything had passed through, two of the remaining handful of legionaries shut the gates of the fort. The fact that some of Sulla's men had been left behind presented Rhidian with a problem. How could he get his tribe into the fort without the legionaries noticing? The presence of a nearby storage building, with a door bolted on the outside, gave the boy an idea.

Leaving Valeria safely in hiding, Rhidian ran out into

the fort compound and deliberately attracted the attention of the two legionaries who, by now, were on the ramparts near the gate. They soon left their positions and gave chase. The boy ran into the storage building he had earlier noted and waited behind the door until the legionaries came in after him. Then he darted back out of the door and bolted it securely so that his pursuers were trapped on the inside.

With the ramparts of the fort now clear, Rhidian sprinted over to the gates and, with some difficulty, opened them. It required only a brief hand-signal to attract the attention of the people of the Ewenni tribe, who had been waiting in the woods outside. They emerged from their positions immediately and, with Trojan the stallion following on behind, headed for the fort. Once inside, the tribesfolk set to work rooting out, and then restraining, the remaining few legionaries in their barracks.

Meanwhile, Rhidian returned to the site of the devastated bird shed to find Valeria sitting on the rubble in a mood of considerable gloom.

"What's the matter?" asked the boy. "Don't you know what's about to happen? We must leave quickly if there's to be a chance of helping the Gwenfo tribe against Sulla."

"It's no use," said Valeria, miserably. "Our only hope lay with the Roman army that was sent to besiege the Dinas. If their commander, Darius, could have been persuaded to turn against Sulla and to take our side instead, then we might have stood a chance of helping our friends. As things are, the situation is hopeless. I mean, we don't even have the pigeon."

"Pigeon?" inquired Rhidian. "Would that be the one Sulla was holding before the explosion?"

"Exactly."

The boy shook his head, sadly. "I nearly managed to catch that bird; but, at the last moment, it slipped out of my hand."

"Slipped out of your hand?" echoed Valeria, with some irritation. "Do you mean that you had the chance of catching the creature, and didn't? Couldn't you see how important it was?"

"I am sure that if the bird is as important as you say, then the Lord will make it known to us."

"Did you say '*us*'?" Aren't you forgetting something? *You* may believe in the Lord, but *I* don't. I'm not a follower of the Way."

"I was afraid of that. It explains what happened in my dream."

"Your dream?"

"Last night, on the mountain, I had visions in my sleep. They were all about you – I'm sure of it – and about what will happen to you if you refuse to become a follower of the Way. In the dream, there was this creature: a black beast. It was poised to attack you; it wanted *you*, Valeria. But the creature wasn't just in my dream; there was a *real* one too, out there on the mountain. I saw it. And now I think I know what it means.

214

Whatever the beast in my dream represents, it is as real as the creature on the mountain was. Accept the Lord Jesus and become a follower of the Way, Valeria, before it's too late . . ."

Valeria started to laugh. "Real beasts, imaginary beasts. I knew it. You don't know the difference between what's real and imaginary any more. If that's what being a follower of the Way is all about, I shall be leaving it well alone."

Rhidian felt hurt. "Sulla would understand the meaning of what I saw in my dream – he would understand it only too well. Don't you remember what he told you just before leaving you to the mercy of that explosion? He said he had no doubt that when you passed from this world to the other side, you would have your audience with the *being who lies behind the mask of Mithras*. What do you think Sulla meant by that?"

"I don't know."

"Yes you do. He was speaking of the . . ."

"Not now, Rhidian. Can't we talk about it later? After all, I haven't even had a moment to . . . thank you for rescuing me yet . . ."

A strange look flickered across Valeria's face. Slowly, but with unflinching determination, she reached out, placed her arms around the boy and began to kiss him with intensity and persistence. Rhidian was speechless. He felt drawn to return Valeria's advances and yet something held him back. It was not that he had never wished to be an object of the girl's affections, for indeed he had; it was simply that the timing of Valeria's embrace seemed premature – an idle distraction at a moment when there were so many matters left unresolved, not to mention the girl's failure to become a follower of the Way. Rhidian's sense of unease must have become evident to Valeria, for she soon stopped hugging the boy and sheepishly sat down at the side of him.

"I'm sorry," she murmured. "It's too late, you see. Nothing matters now. We don't have the pigeon . . . can't help the Gwenfo tribe . . ."

For some time, neither Rhidian nor Valeria said a word. The silence was soon broken, however, by someone shouting from the far side of the fort. It turned out that the voice in question belonged to Rhidian's father, Elgan. Moments later, he came running up to explain that all the remaining legionaries in the fort had been rounded up and locked away. What was more, some horses had been found together with a variety of weapons which, it was suggested, might now be turned against Sulla.

"Oh, and by the way," Elgan added, "we found this . . ."

When Valeria saw what Rhidian's father was referring to, she leapt to her feet with excitement – for Elgan was carrying in his hand a pigeon. The question was: could this bird be the one that had been sent by Constantius? Her fingers visibly trembling, Valeria felt for anything that might be attached to the pigeon's legs. Sure enough, she soon found a message. Opening it up, the girl then read the contents out loud:

*"In case of confusion, those who have occasion to observe this communication are advised that the Imperial Inspectorate of Mines has no jurisdiction over the people of the hill tribes. Therefore, if it should prove to be the case that the Head of the Inspectorate, Decurio Sulla, is either engaged in, or is contemplating, an unprovoked attack against any such tribe, he is to be stopped by whatever means may be considered necessary. Our long-standing policy of avoiding unnecessary conflict with the indigenous peoples of the Cambrian Region must not be compromised.*

*"By Order of Constantius."*

"What more do we need!" cried Rhidian, excitedly. "The words speak for themselves. All we have to do now is to reach that fellow, Darius, at the Dinas and hand him the message. Sulla will have to call off the siege then."

"You're forgetting one thing," said Valeria. "If we're to do any good, we would have to reach the Dinas before Sulla does, or else he'll see to it that we don't get anywhere near Darius. The trouble is, the Decurio has a head-start on us; I don't see how we can get in front of him now."

"There's still a chance," observed Elgan. "I saw which way Sulla went when he left the fort. He chose the Claerwen Route which will take him round the

217

south flank of Mallaen. Now that is not the fastest way to the Dinas. The route that leads through the Beddau Pass is far quicker."

"Of course!" exclaimed Valeria. "With all those men, and that heavy equipment, Sulla would have needed to use the Claerwen Route – it is the widest and smoothest trail available."

"If all this is true," declared Rhidian, "we must head for the Beddau Pass at once. Then it may still be possible to reach the Dinas ahead of Sulla and cut him off from Darius."

It seemed that Rhidian had voiced the conclusion that everyone had now reached. All those in the fort compound who were able to do so found horses to ride on. Rhidian and Valeria took Trojan, the stallion, for the creature had, of course, been waiting patiently beside the gates ever since Elgan had brought her in. Then the whole company, including some two dozen members of the Ewenni tribe, galloped out of the fort and into the wilderness, all of them intent on a common purpose: to reach the Dinas before Sulla.

CHAPTER FOURTEEN

# Battle at the Dinas

With Trojan, the stallion, out in front, the column of horses pounded up the Cothi Valley as far as the Dam. Here the riders struck the trail leading past the marbled pillars of the Mithras Temple; but with the uncomfortable memory of what had happened there still fresh in his mind, Rhidian resolved not to give the place so much as a sideways glance.

Inevitably, the steep gradient of the track leading to the Beddau Pass made it difficult for the horses to keep up the pace that was demanded of them; and even when they began to descend into the Vale of the Llyfnant, there were further obstacles – the rocky terrain where the infamous landslide had once occurred and the low-lying branches in the dense woodland beyond. Eventually, however, as the valley began to widen out and the trails became more clearly defined, the riders were able to sit high in their saddles and spur their horses on once more.

By this point, they were within the familiar tribal territory of the Ewenni, a fact that seemed to have an uplifting effect on everyone's morale. Even so, when the column reached the place where the waters of the Llyfnant flowed into the Towy, Rhidian felt distinctly uneasy; for he knew that this was the point where the trails from the Cothi and Claerwen Passes converged and where, consequently, there was the greatest danger of colliding with Sulla and his men.

Despite this concern, however, there were no immediate signs of trouble. The riders were able to cross the Towy River without incident and to join the main trail to the Dinas unhindered. Only then, when they had reached a point some two miles south of their destination, did circumstances change. The first Rhidian knew of it was when he heard someone shouting from behind. It was the boy's father, near the back of the column, who confirmed what everyone must have been dreading.

"Fly at once!" cried Elgan. "It is the enemy!"

No-one needed to be warned twice. Valeria spurred Trojan on while Rhidian clung on behind as best he could. The boy cast a fearful glance over his shoulder. Sure enough, there, less than a field's length away, was a large army; and some of the horsemen at the front appeared to be gaining fast on the Ewenni tribe.

"Don't wait for us!" shouted Elgan to Rhidian and Valeria. "Ride on ahead and give your message to Darius – that's what counts. We'll try to distract Sulla."

The thought of leaving his tribe in the path of the

advancing army did not in the least appeal to Rhidian; but he was in no position to argue, for the horse on which he sat was already being driven well ahead of the rest of the column by a determined Valeria.

The rocky pinnacle of the Dinas, having already been visible for some time, was now drawing tantalisingly close. Darius could not be too far away, but would it be possible to reach him in time? Already, a number of Sulla's horsemen – three of them, in all – were galloping ahead of the rest and had caught up with some of the riders at the back of the Ewenni column.

For Rhidian, the first sign of activity up ahead came when Trojan rounded a final bend on the river. There, in the meadows just below the Dinas, could be seen a large body of legionaries – all of them, no doubt, Darius's men. Some of them were seated around a camp fire. When they turned and saw what was coming in their direction, they leapt to their feet abruptly. The boy already had the order from Constantius in his hand, and was all set to deliver it, when disaster struck.

A gust of wind suddenly caught the piece of parchment, snatching it from Rhidian's grasp. Instinctively, the boy lunged out in an effort to retrieve the order but, in doing so, he lost his balance and, to his horror, found himself falling off Trojan's back. The next few moments passed by in a blur of confusion. Rhidian struck the ground almost immediately but it took much longer for his body to come to rest, rolling as it did through the long grass of the meadow.

Incredibly, the boy was left feeling more dazed than injured by his fall; but at such a time, even to be dazed was a luxury that Rhidian could not afford. He could see that Valeria, by this point, had noticed what had happened and was beginning to turn Trojan round. However, the girl was now some distance away. It seemed doubtful that she would be able to return quickly enough to help Rhidian. Even so, the boy picked himself up and did what he knew to be vital – he ran back to retrieve Constantius's order.

The piece of parchment stood out clearly enough against the grass, but even as he picked it up Rhidian saw one of Sulla's horsemen appear at the end of the meadow. Somehow, this one rider had managed to move ahead of the Ewenni tribe. Rhidian turned and began to run as fast as he could towards Valeria who, by now, was fast approaching from the opposite direction; but by the time the two of them had met, Sulla's horseman was almost upon them.

It was clear that Rhidian would be unable to mount Trojan safely at that moment and so the boy raced on towards Darius's men, shouting to Valeria to do the same. Valeria, however, plainly had other ideas, for she quickly attempted to divert the enemy rider. The effort met with little success. That the man really wished to stop Rhidian, and no-one else, soon became plain from his tactics. At every attempt by Valeria to place herself in his way, the rider simply dodged past.

Rhidian was now less than perhaps fifty strides from

Darius's encampment. One of the men within the camp could plainly be seen walking out into the centre of the meadow with what looked like the standard of the legion in his hand. He planted the object in the ground and then stood back as if to wait for Rhidian's arrival.

"It's Darius himself!" yelled Valeria. "You know what to do Rhid!"

Rhidian did indeed know what to do, but could he do it in time? The boy was running at full stretch, all too conscious of the fact that, just behind him, Sulla's rider had now pulled past Valeria. Indeed, the pounding of the horse's hooves was drawing terrifyingly close. Within moments, Rhidian felt something whistle past his ear and then Sulla's rider thundered past, sword in hand.

The man, evidently aware of the fact that Rhidian was still running, turned his horse around and came back for a second pass. This time, however, the boy was ready. At the last moment, he was able to jump to one side and avoid the rider's charge.

Rhidian could see that the object he had earlier observed being placed in the centre of the meadow was indeed the standard of a legion, for it was now just a few paces away from him. With one last burst of energy, the boy shot past the standard and, with the order from Constantius protruding from his hand, dropped to the ground, exhausted, at Darius's feet.

Darius reached down and prised the piece of parchment from Rhidian's fingers; but before the Tribune had a chance to read the order, Sulla's rider came thundering along.

"I'll take that," he said, putting out his hand for the parchment.

"You'll do no such thing," came the response. "At least, not until I have *read* the message; for it is clear, is it not, that the boy intended it for *my* perusal and not for yours."

Seemingly stung by the rebuff, Sulla's representative sat glowering in his saddle for some moments until Darius had read the order from Constantius.

"Well?" demanded the rider, finally. "What am I to tell my Master?"

"Tell him he's not welcome here!" shouted Valeria, as she came galloping up over the meadow. "And that if he tries to attack the Dinas, he'll be sorry! What do you say, Darius?"

"I say," replied the Tribune, grimly, "that this is no place for a young lady and certainly not for one who has made an enemy of the Decurio. Now, take your friend here and head for the Dinas. I shall speak with Sulla myself – he will be here soon enough."

It was true. Already, Rhidian could see the Decurio coming into view at the far end of the meadow with the first of his legionaries. Just ahead of them were the Ewenni tribe, galloping out in front for all they were worth. When they saw Darius and his men, however, they began to veer off to one side, perhaps out of a misguided concern that they might be heading into a trap.

It was only a series of frantic gestures from Rhidian that finally seemed to persuade them that they could continue straight ahead. Soon, the Ewenni had joined Rhidian and Valeria next to Darius's encampment.

At the same time, however, the Tribune and those under his command had been moving in the opposite direction – they had now taken up defensive positions further down the meadow in anticipation of Sulla's arrival. So it was that when Sulla finally rode up, he was faced with a solid line of resistance.

As more and more of the Decurio's men poured into the meadow, however, the enormity of the forces ranged against Darius became all too evident. It was a fact that could not have been lost on the unfortunate Tribune himself – so much so that Rhidian fully expected the man to back down at once. Instead, an argument took place; at least, this was what it looked like to Rhidian. Darius appeared to be pointing insistently at the object he still held in his hand – the order from Constantius. Sulla then began to raise his voice in protest. The exchange soon became so heated that the Decurio finally lost his patience, turned his horse around and galloped back down the meadow to rejoin the main body of his army.

From their vantage point on the trail to the Dinas, Rhidian and the others stared at the unfolding scene behind them with a growing sense of horror; for they could see what was about to happen, and happen it did. To the sound of a piercing battle-cry, Sulla raised his sword and charged forwards with his legionaries behind him. Darius's men responded immediately by firing off a hail of arrows. Yet this did little to impede the advance of the enemy and, finally, the two sides clashed head-on. Swords sliced through the air and flashed in the sunlight to the grim echoes of battle. Darius put up a determined defence but the onslaught against him was ferocious.

"What can we do?" wailed Valeria. "If this continues, Darius will be crushed."

"Unless . . . ," murmured Rhidian, "unless Sulla can be crushed first . . ."

"And just how are we going to achieve *that*?"

"I have an idea; but before it will work, there is something we must find!"

Bidding his companions to follow him, Rhidian raced along the trail that led past the *Pool of the Mingled Woad*. That the area around the West Door of the Dinas had been visited by Darius and his men seemed evident from the many sandal footprints left in the ground thereabouts. The entrance itself, however, appeared to have remained undisturbed; for when Rhidian passed into the basket chasm, he quickly found what he was looking for and, with great excitement, held it up for all to see.

Valeria turned pale.

"Well?" inquired the boy. "Aren't you going to help me with this? It's just a barrel of . . . Cambrian Powder."

"I know," muttered Valeria, miserably. "That's the problem."

"Problem? I don't understand. If we use it properly, this barrel could win us the battle against Sulla!"

Valeria sank heavily to the ground. "You don't know what it was like back at the fort – being trapped in that bird-house with the powder there; and then, when the barrel finally exploded . . . what a terrible thing that substance is, Rhidian! Do we really have to use it?"

Rhidian sighed deeply. He thought for a moment and then, taking his father to one side, whispered some instructions in his ear.

"Don't forget," said Rhidian, finally, "wait for my signal before you do anything."

With that, the boy took the Cambrian Powder and hurriedly bundled a nervous-looking Valeria into the basket at the bottom of the chasm. After the two of them had been raised to the top, by means of the lifting mechanism, the girl still seemed less than her usual self. The situation was not helped by the fact that the expected welcome by the Gwenfo folk failed to materialise. Indeed, the nearby passages of the Dinas seemed completely deserted.

Rhidian reached across to Valeria and took her hand. She was visibly trembling.

"Now listen," said the boy, firmly, "I can set the powder off on my own, but it must be done without delay if it's to be of any use to Darius. Can you do something for me? Find Aaron, Eifiona and the others. Tell them what's happening down below. Oh, and by the way, ask them to pray for the Lord's guidance in all we do today. I have a feeling that we shall be needing it."

"Speak for yourself," replied Valeria, irritably. "I don't believe in that sort of thing – I'm not a follower of the Way, don't forget."

"So you keep telling me."

Bidding Valeria a hurried farewell, Rhidian set off through the tunnels of the Dinas as fast as his hefty barrel of Cambrian Powder would allow. He chose a steep passage that took him past the familiar cave known as the Manuscript Vault. Once he had reached the summit of the Dinas, Rhidian headed straight for a certain point. It overshadowed what he knew to be a treacherous, landslide-prone flank of the mountain. From here, Elgan, Gwawr and most of the Ewenni tribe could be seen standing near the bottom of a large deposit of scree down below. Most noticeable of all, however, was the scene further down the valley where Darius and his men were clearly struggling to hold back the forces of Sulla. Already, the battle-field was peppered with the bodies of the fallen – and still the Decurio kept advancing. It was up to Rhidian now to prevent the retreat of Darius from becoming a complete disaster.

The first thing the boy did was to give the pre-arranged signal to Elgan. If everything now proceeded according to the plan Rhidian had discussed with his father, it was only a matter of time before the barrel of Cambrian Powder would be needed. Rhidian watched while one of the Ewenni tribesmen was dispatched to the battle-field. The man could soon be seen communicating with the nearest of Darius's legionaries. Then Rhidian noticed the first signs of what he had been wanting to see: a retreat.

From his position high above the valley, the boy looked on while the legionaries nearest the Dinas began to back off up the meadow and onto the trails leading in the direction of the *Woad*. The rest of Darius's men soon followed, while attempting to maintain their defences against Sulla. This was clearly no easy task for them – moving, as they now were, on stony ground. Rhidian waited anxiously while the legionaries crossed the area below the scree slope of the Dinas. Finally, when the last of them began to disappear from view off to the right, the boy knew that the moment he had been waiting for had arrived.

Trembling with apprehension, Rhidian ran across to a particularly unstable-looking group of rocks lying just next to the summit precipice. He felt sure that if these objects could be made to move, they would quickly set off many more, thereby causing a large fall of debris in just the right place down below. The boy therefore wedged the Cambrian Powder in among the rocks and, with his pieces of flint, and tinder-box, to hand, lit the tallowed wick above the barrel. He then ducked down behind some nearby bushes to await the result.

The explosion, when it came, seemed quieter than the boy had expected. Whether this was due simply to his position in relation to the blast, or to something more serious, was not immediately apparent; but what did seem clear, when Rhidian stood up to observe it, was that none of the rocks in the vicinity of the explosion had moved at all. The plan had failed!

The boy rushed over to the edge of the summit to see what was happening down below. Already the leading column of Sulla's army was beginning to draw past the scree slopes. In no time at all, they would be out of range of any falling debris and free to continue their massacre of Darius's men. Indeed, it occurred to Rhidian that by encouraging his Roman friends to withdraw up the valley, he might even have made the task of the enemy easier. In desperation, Rhidian tried to start a landslide with his bare hands by pushing some nearby boulders over the edge of the summit; but despite these efforts, no significant mass movement of rocks took place.

The boy was about to tear back down through the tunnels of the Dinas to do what he could for his friends down below when something unexpected happened. The ground began to quake – almost imperceptibly at first, but with growing intensity as the moments passed. When a number of cracks began to appear in the rocks at the edge of the summit, Rhidian finally realised what was happening: the south-west flank of the mountain was becoming unstable. It suddenly seemed that the blasting effect of the Cambrian Powder might have achieved something after all. The boy watched with astonishment as an entire section of the summit began to part company with the rest, tilting precariously for a moment before falling away completely. Rhidian moved as close as he dared to the edge and stared into the abyss.

A vast quantity of rock, dislodged from the face of the Dinas, could be seen crashing into the valley below. Sulla would have had little warning. Within a few short moments, the bulk of his army had been consumed beneath the rubble of the landslide.

The dust cloud caused by the falling debris took some time to disperse but, when it did, it soon became clear that Darius now had the advantage over the enemy. Those of Sulla's men who had survived the landslide eventually surrendered although not without attempting to escape back down the valley first. Rhidian watched these developments with a growing sense of relief. In fact, he was about to go and join his friends down below when a noise from somewhere nearby startled him. It sounded like someone shouting from inside the Dinas.

Thinking that the disturbance might be something to do with Valeria, Rhidian raced back down into the tunnels of the Dinas. He had retraced his steps to a point approaching the Manuscript Vault when he began to smell smoke. A few feet further down the passage and the boy was able to see into the cave where the sacred scrolls were kept. He was horrified by the scene that greeted him. Some of the manuscripts were on fire!

231

What was more, if something wasn't done immediately, everything in the Vault would soon go up in flames!

Rhidian ran into the cave, picked up one of the many buckets of water that lay on the floor and threw the contents over the burning manuscripts. To the boy's great relief, the fire was soon extinguished. As the last of the flames spluttered into oblivion, it was clear that, but for Rhidian's prompt arrival in the Vault, the damage caused to the work of the Gwenfo folk would have been of incalculable proportions.

While the boy stood taking in the scene around him, he heard a sound from over his shoulder. He spun round and, to his astonishment, caught sight of the very person he would least have expected to see at that moment – it was Sulla! Just how the man had managed to enter the Dinas, and yet avoid being captured by Darius, was unclear; but it now seemed all too obvious that it had been the Decurio who had set the scrolls alight.

To Rhidian's surprise, Sulla made no attempt to stand and fight. In fact, he scurried out of the cave and darted into the passage leading off to the left. Rhidian began to chase after him but, as the boy ran out of the Vault, he almost collided with Valeria who happened to be rushing up the tunnel from the right. The girl had evidently been trying to pursue Sulla herself.

"To the summit!" cried Rhidian. "That's where he's going."

Valeria nodded fervently. "Aaron and the others are

on their way; Darius and his men should be here soon, too. They'll deal with Sulla if we can show them where he is. We mustn't lose him!"

But lose him they did. By the time Rhidian and Valeria had reached the summit of the Dinas, the Decurio was nowhere to be seen. It was clear that he had to have gone somewhere on the mountain-top; but where? Rhidian had almost decided to return back down the passages of the Dinas to try and find help when suddenly, without warning, Sulla leapt out from behind a rock. Before anyone had a chance to say anything, the Decurio seized Valeria and put his sword up against her throat.

"I have been sorely tried this day by the two of you!" he rasped. "And for that, the life of the girl shall be forfeit. By the powers of Mithras, and the blood of the bull, may it be so!"

"Wait!" cried Rhidian, his thoughts racing. "If you will spare the girl's life, I can help you to escape."

"To escape, boy? Why should I wish to do that? Is there not glory in martyrdom?"

"That depends on the cause of the martyr. If I were you, I would be looking for glory somewhere else; and you can't do that unless you escape from this mountain."

"And how might that be done, pray? The passages down below will be full of Darius's men; and, as for climbing down the sides of this mountain, they are surely too steep . . ."

"That leaves only one possibility. Come, let me show you."

"Have a care, boy! I am quick with the sword."

Followed by a suspicious-looking Sulla, and his reluctant hostage, Rhidian made haste across to the south-east side of the summit, to the place that was so familiar to him from the previous day – the launch site of the *cherubim*. There, still under cover, were the two remaining pairs of Towser's wings. Already showing signs of impatience, the Decurio's expression changed to one of disbelief when he saw what Rhidian had in mind.

"You want me to *fly* one of those things? It would be madness, boy! Have you not heard the Greek tale of Icarus and the wings that melted in the sun?"

"There is no sun today," replied Rhidian.

"And," added Valeria, "remember that man Daedalus in the story? He flew successfully."

Sulla pressed his sword ever more firmly to Valeria's neck.

"You have my word," insisted Rhidian, quickly. "These wings work – I have tried them myself."

For some moments, Sulla seemed lost in thought. It was the sound of men shouting from somewhere down inside the Dinas that finally appeared to bring him to a decision.

"Very well, boy. Show me these wings; and no tricks, or my blade shall taste blood!"

Without delay, Rhidian pulled the nearest *cherub*

into position near the top of the angled slab of rock that had been used the day before as a launching chute. Sulla was then hurriedly given some instructions on how to operate the craft. When he had been told all that there was to know, he quickly agreed to release Valeria, pushed her across to Rhidian and then clambered into the *cherub*. Without so much as a glance backwards, the Decurio began to shunt himself towards the precipice. As he did so, it became clear that his craft was shifting sideways to such an extent that it could not take a straight dive down the launch chute.

In a final effort to be rid of their adversary, Rhidian and Valeria took hold of the tail-end of the *cherub* and began to haul it back into the correct position; but before the task could be completed, Sulla unexpectedly started to shunt his craft forwards once more. It was a move that had disastrous consequences. Somehow, Valeria lost her balance and was dragged along in the wake of the *cherub*. She had no time to disentangle herself. As the craft finally cleared the edge of the summit, and took to the air, the girl was forced to hang on underneath.

CHAPTER FIFTEEN

# The River Runs Red

R hidian had witnessed the rapid sequence of events with horror. His reaction was instinctive. He dashed across to the one remaining *cherub*, hauled it into position, and seated himself at the controls. Within moments, the boy was airborne and combing the expanse below him for signs of Sulla's craft. He soon spotted it, but was alarmed to see how far it had dropped – hundreds of feet in just a few moments. From such a distance, and elevation, it was impossible to tell how Sulla and Valeria had fared; but Rhidian was determined to find out.

He angled his wings and tail section in such a way as to ensure a rapid descent and then, by adopting a spiralling manoeuvre, was eventually able to bring himself into a position slightly above and behind the craft he was pursuing. At this point, the boy could see, to his great relief, that Valeria was still hanging on below Sulla's seat, though her position seemed far from secure. Indeed, the Decurio was doing his best to try and kick the girl off her only means of support.

Rhidian responded immediately. He put his *cherub* into a dive with the intention of coming up directly beneath Sulla. It seemed an impossible task, not least because the craft in front was constantly lurching from side to side. Moreover, by the time the boy had moved into a position just beneath Valeria, the ground seemed to be drawing uncomfortably close.

Owing to the rate at which the two craft had descended, neither Sulla nor his pursuer had flown far from the immediate vicinity of the Dinas. In effect, the chase had at first taken a southerly course but had then veered back to the north, past the western flank of the mountain. As a result, Rhidian soon found himself struggling to avoid a collision with the enormous mound of rubble from the earlier landslide. Meanwhile, Sulla shot past overhead with his unwelcome passenger still in tow.

Once Rhidian had cleared the site of the landslide, he was able to see what lay not far beyond it: the *Pool of the Mingled Woad* – the place where the waters of the Towy and Doethia met. The boy glanced apprehensively at the wings of his *cherub*. It occurred to him that if there was such a thing as a safe landing in such a craft, then a touch-down on water had to offer the best chance of it. The idea seemed to have occurred to Sulla also, for he quickly gave up trying to dislodge Valeria and, instead, began to nudge his *cherub* in a direction that would take him down over the *Woad*. Valeria had only to hold on for a few more moments and she would be able to drop safely into the water.

That, at least, was how things appeared to Rhidian, until he swooped closer to the edge of the pool. Only then did he notice that something was amiss. The volume of water flowing downstream seemed far greater than the boy remembered it to have been; but that was not all. Gone was the pale-green hue that had once characterised the pool. Now its surface was infused with the shades of a very different colour: red.

It was a circumstance that caused Rhidian to panic, for he had suddenly remembered Aaron's remarks concerning the peculiar properties of the *Woad* and of its capacity to change colour under certain conditions. When the waters ran red, the pedlar had emphasised, it indicated that one of the rivers entering the pool had burst its banks high in the mountains, bringing red particles of iron ore downstream. Under such circumstances, the prevailing currents in the *Woad* would be reversed, causing a treacherous vortex to appear. Sure enough, as Rhidian looked down from above, he could see pieces of floating debris being dragged inexorably from the edges of the pool towards the centre.

However, it was what Aaron had said about human victims of the vortex that preyed on Rhidian's mind most of all; for it had transpired that the fate of those who entered the *Woad* depended upon their spiritual condition – whether they were believers in Christ or not. A believer, it was said, would emerge from the pool unscathed; an unbeliever, on the other hand, would fail to escape the clutches of the vortex, with fearsome consequences for the eternal destiny of the individual concerned. If this was the case, as Aaron had insisted it was, then the implications for Sulla would be dire indeed; for if the Decurio was not an example of an unbeliever, it seemed difficult to imagine who was.

Rhidian looked on with a sense of foreboding as Sulla's *cherub* passed over the surface of the *Woad*. Fearful for Valeria's safety, the boy shouted to his friend to jump into calmer waters around the edges of the pool, rather than risk splashing down near the vortex. She seemed to take heed, finally dropping from the *cherub* just as her feet began to graze the surface of the *Woad*.

Still seated in his craft, Sulla was soon ploughing a furrow through the waters of the pool, to be followed, moments later, by Rhidian. Having had the advantage of a lighter load than his adversary, the boy had been able to bring his *cherub* down gently. He was therefore in a position to guide the craft into the banks of the pool, where it was soon grounded next to a fallen tree trunk.

Sulla had been less fortunate. The wings of his *cherub* had been twisted out of shape by the force of impact on splashing-down; they were already being drawn towards the vortex at the centre of the pool. The Decurio, meanwhile, lost no time in abandoning his craft. He leapt into the water and, much to the boy's disquiet, began to strike out for the area of bank where

Rhidian was situated. Since it was the nearest piece of dry land for all concerned, Valeria seemed to have decided to swim the same way.

Not wishing to leave the scene with his friend still in the pool, Rhidian was in a quandary as to what he should do. Within moments, Sulla had reached the fallen tree trunk at the water's edge. It was then that the boy noticed something strange. Wrapped around Sulla's leg could be seen a length of cord. It had evidently worked itself loose from the Decurio's *cherub*, for part of it was still attached to the wings of the craft. Moreover, as the floating wreckage moved nearer the vortex, the slackness in the cord was rapidly diminishing. If Sulla couldn't disentangle himself in time, he would soon be pulled backwards with the *cherub*.

"Well, boy," he shouted, "if you were truly a follower of the Way, you would assist your enemy in his hour of need."

"I intend to," replied the boy, "but not in the way you might think. I have some advice. If you wish to live, and to escape from this pool, then you must repent of your sins."

"Repent? And become a follower of the Way? What foolishness is this?"

"If you do not confess that Jesus is Lord, you will perish in these waters and face the wrath of God."

"Nonsense, boy! Just give me your hand. That's all I . . ."

Sulla's voice broke off abruptly. As the wreckage of

the *cherub* finally disappeared into the vortex, the cord attached to the Decurio's leg suddenly became taut. Sulla was now desperately struggling to keep grip of the branch he was holding so as to avoid being dragged backwards. His efforts were in vain; but just as the branch slipped through his fingers, Valeria came swimming along. She was on the point of reaching out for a branch herself when the Decurio somehow managed to catch hold of her ankles. She began to scream for help. If Rhidian didn't act immediately, his friend would be dragged into the vortex along with Sulla.

The boy waded into the water, holding onto the fallen tree trunk with one hand and reaching out to Valeria with the other. The girl needed no prompting; she seized Rhidian's hand at once. However, if she had thought it possible to escape from the pool easily, her hopes were to be dashed; for the Decurio was still clinging firmly to her heels. Rhidian's arms were already beginning to ache. Although positioned at the edge of the pool, he could feel the force of the vortex being passed on to him through Sulla and Valeria. The question was: whose strength would fail first?

"Be warned, boy," snarled Sulla, "if this accursed pool is to claim *my* life, it shall take the life of your friend also!"

"Not if I can help it!" cried Rhidian. "The vortex is a danger only to those who do not believe in Christ."

"If you are right, then Valeria is as doomed as I am; for the girl is an unbeliever, like me."

"That," said Rhidian, grimly, "is why my friend has a decision to make; and quickly. What do you say, Valeria?"

Valeria grimaced. "Not now, Rhid, . . . I can't think."

"That's right," chimed Sulla, "the girl needs time to think."

"There, you see, Valeria?" said Rhidian, desperately. "If you don't make a decision, then you're siding with the enemy."

"Look, all I want to do is to get out of the water!"

"First, you must confess that Jesus is . . ."

"Yes, I know what to say."

"Then say it; and mean it!"

"Stop!" boomed Sulla. "If you do this, young lady, I shall see to it that you will for evermore be pursued by the vengeful spirits and minions of Mithras."

"Don't listen to him," cried Rhidian. "He has no power over you unless you let him have it."

Before Rhidian had a chance to say any more, Valeria suddenly slipped from his grasp and disappeared beneath the surface of the pool. Horrified, the boy began clutching at the water in a desperate attempt to find his friend – but to no avail. It quickly became all too clear what must have happened. Sulla's *cherub*, which was no longer visible, had evidently been dragged down into the vortex. The cord trailing from it, that was caught around the Decurio's leg, would then have been pulled under the water, taking Sulla and Valeria down too.

Rhidian dived into the pool, searching frantically for any signs of life; but the foaming currents made it difficult to see anything either above or below the waves. Indeed, the conditions were such that the boy was struggling to control his own movements. If he ventured any further out into the pool, the currents would become too strong for him.

While Rhidian was flailing around in the water, he suddenly caught sight of Sulla up ahead. There was no mistaking the fate that awaited the Decurio. Having been pulled to the middle of the pool, his body was being spun round the mouth of the vortex like a pebble on a string – and the string was becoming shorter by the moment. What was more, all kinds of objects that happened to be in the water were being drawn into the centre of the *Woad* by the powerful currents there. Circling the vortex were a number of what looked like Roman swords, and other weapons, that had presumably been swept into the pool by the earlier landslide.

Just how it happened, Rhidian was not sure; but, suddenly, the Decurio let out the most fearsome cry. The blades that had been tearing through the water had finally found a target – in Sulla. It was as if a number of invisible legionaries had instantaneously sunk their swords into him, for the wounds, and the weapons that had caused them, were plainly to be seen in his body. There could be no escape for the Decurio now. With one last roar of defiance, his fist clenched in a gesture of rage, Sulla disappeared into the vortex. He was gone.

It should have been a moment of great rejoicing, or perhaps simply one of relief. In fact, neither of these sentiments could have described Rhidian's mood. It was true that his greatest foe had been vanquished, but at what cost? To have lost his greatest friend in the process seemed an unbearably high price to have paid; yet that was surely the terrible implication of what had happened. For if Valeria had survived, Rhidian would have expected her, by this point, to have reappeared somewhere on the surface of the *Woad*. The fact that she had not done so seemed ominous in the extreme.

With a heavy heart, Rhidian swam back to the fallen tree trunk and climbed out of the pool. He tried calling out for Valeria, but there was no response – nothing to break the constant sound of the waters pounding in the *Woad*.

The boy slumped down on the pebbles beside the pool in despair. Never had he thought that events would come to this: that Valeria would be taken from him at the last moment. Rhidian had known the girl for but a brief space of time, and yet she had come to mean more to him than he would have thought possible at the moment of his first encounter. There had been something elusive about Valeria's manner and personality that had quite captivated the boy. Now there would never be a chance to explore its depths.

Yet it was for Valeria herself that Rhidian felt the greatest anguish. The boy's attempts to bring his friend to a knowledge of the Lord appeared to have failed completely. To Rhidian, the implications seemed almost too dreadful to contemplate; but contemplate them, he did. Why, oh why, had Valeria not taken the opportunity, while she was still able, to accept the Lord as her Saviour? The fact that she had not done so had seemingly condemned her to the same fate as Sulla.

Rhidian had been agonising over these questions for only a short space of time when something – he knew not what – made him look up. As the boy glanced across the pool, his attention was drawn to a movement on the opposite bank. A man, dressed in the costume of a Roman legionary, was standing there. He appeared to be gesturing frantically in Rhidian's direction. Thinking that it might be one of Darius's men in need of assistance, the boy stirred himself and, although he did not feel in a fit state to help anyone, made haste to the far side of the pool.

The legionary turned out to be a tall, flaxen-haired individual whose weapons and armour seemed strangely free of the blood and grime that might have been expected of one of Darius's battle-worn warriors.

"Well, lad," began the man, cheerfully, "have you no welcome for a messenger of the Lord?"

"Messenger of the Lord?" inquired Rhidian, cautiously. "Are you a follower of the Way, then?"

The stranger chuckled. "You could say that – you could indeed! For it is my task to attend to those who are to be saved."

"Then you are here to help *me*?"

"Not exactly. You see, there is someone else who is in rather more urgent need of help than you are. Indeed, she is on the point of death."

"Did you say 'she'? Rhidian stared at the stranger with a growing sense of unease. "You are speaking of Valeria, aren't you? Where is she? I must see her."

The stranger nodded, sympathetically, and then began to walk into a nearby patch of woodland, beckoning Rhidian to follow. Soon, the two of them had reached a clearing among the trees. There, lying on the ground with her eyes closed, was Valeria. Just how long she had been resting there was unclear, but her body seemed pale and limp. What was far worse, however, she appeared to have stopped breathing. Greatly alarmed, Rhidian knelt down and listened for a heart beat; that too was absent. In desperation, the boy turned to the stranger, hoping for guidance, but the man had begun to walk away.

"There's still time, lad," he observed calmly. "You can do it. I have seen it done by the people of your own tribe. All the girl requires is air flowing in her lungs and blood pumping through her heart . . ."

Rhidian felt he knew what the stranger was referring to: the practice of reviving a person who had fallen unconscious; but would it work in this case? Although the boy had once seen someone being revived, he was by no means sure that he himself had the ability to perform the task; and was there not a danger that the girl might be injured still further in the process?

Apprehensively, Rhidian laid Valeria flat on the ground and, tilting her head slightly backwards, began to breathe air into her lungs. He quickly attempted to restore the girl's heart-beat by repeatedly jolting her chest with his hands. Yet Valeria still showed no signs of recovery.

These were anxious moments for Rhidian. Was the boy perhaps doing something wrong? Had the stranger – the self-styled messenger of the Lord – lied in suggesting that Valeria could be roused? Had Rhidian been brought to this place only to bid his friend a final farewell? The boy had almost convinced himself that this was indeed the case when something happened to change his mind.

It began with what sounded like a murmur in Valeria's throat. The girl then began to cough and her chest went into convulsions. Rhidian was astonished. It seemed difficult to believe that an apparently lifeless body could have undergone the kind of transformation that Valeria's had. The boy could hardly wait for his friend to open her eyes. What a joy it would be to speak with her again now that the dangers of the past few days were over!

Rhidian had just begun to move Valeria into a more comfortable position when he heard the girl say something.

"Away with you!" she exclaimed. "Be gone, I say, in the name of . . ."

"Valeria," called Rhidian. "Wake up. You must be

having a bad dream or something."

"Oh," said the girl, sounding almost disappointed, "it's you. A pity you weren't around to fend off that creature for me."

"Creature?" inquired the boy. "What creature?"

"The one in my dream. I suppose it would have been rather like the one you saw last night on Mallaen. You told me about it. Remember? It was a large, black cat-like beast – or so you said."

Rhidian froze. If Valeria had indeed seen what she had described, then her ordeal in the pool, and in the moments that followed, had been not merely physical but also spiritual in nature; for the black beast, as Rhidian knew all too well, was a manifestation of the devil.

"Don't worry, Rhid," said Valeria, cheerfully. "The creature went eventually. I persuaded it to leave."

"Persuaded it? How?"

"Let's just say I told it who was Lord."

"You did what?"

"Remember what you told Sulla to say so that he might save himself? I used the very words you gave him."

"But doesn't that mean," said Rhidian, with growing excitement, "that you would have to have become a follower of the Way?"

Valeria folded her arms with an air of contrived indifference. She wore a playful expression on her face as if trying to tease Rhidian into guessing the answer to his own question. Very well, thought the boy. He would play Valeria at her own game.

"You realise," he said, trying not to laugh, "that if you are truly to be a follower of the Way, then the Gwenfo folk will expect you to be baptised in the *Woad*."

Valeria's face fell.

"The sooner we get it done," added the boy, "the better. Are you ready?"

Rhidian made as if to scoop Valeria up off the ground, a move that quickly resulted in violent screams of protest. The boy, meanwhile, pretended to look hurt.

"Have it your own way, then," he complained. "I just thought you might be pleased to take your place beside the rest of us who follow the Way."

"I'm alive, aren't I?" replied Valeria, hotly. "Isn't that enough for you?"

"Not really. You see, I care about your *soul*."

Valeria's eyes glinted with mischief. "Are you sure there isn't some . . . other reason for your interest in me?"

"As it happens," replied Rhidian, suddenly feeling uncomfortable, "there is one other thing; something I haven't spoken about before."

Valeria raised her eyebrows and kept them raised with merciless persistence as Rhidian struggled to choose his words.

"You see," muttered the boy, "a follower of the Way is not meant to be – unequally yoked – which means, among other things, that . . ."

"You're not supposed to marry me unless I am a follower of the Way, like you. Isn't that it?"

Rhidian felt his cheeks beginning to burn. Valeria had clearly anticipated his line of thinking exactly. It occurred to the boy that his friend's recovery from her ordeal in the pool had perhaps been a little too rapid for comfort.

However, before Rhidian had a chance to deal further with the delicate challenge confronting him, there was a great commotion in the woods nearby. Then a large number of people began to appear. First to arrive were Aaron, Eifiona and much of the Gwenfo tribe. Darius's men were not far behind. Then came the Ewenni folk, led by Rhidian's parents, Elgan and Gwawr.

Gwawr marched up to Rhidian and pointed an accusing finger at him.

"A fine frolic you've led us, to be sure!" she declared, reproachfully. "We've been searching high and low. You'd better have a good excuse for your disappearance!"

Aaron began to cough. "If I may be so bold, good lady, is not the dispatch of that great scourge, Sulla, excuse enough for the boy? For that is what your son, and his friend here, have achieved. Take note, all of you. Observe the shades of the *Woad*. It has consumed its victim and no mistake. Sulla is no more!"

"If what you say is true," declared Gwawr, apologetically, "then our Rhidian is a hero indeed."

"A hero indeed!" agreed Elgan, with enthusiasm. "And his friend here too, I shouldn't wonder. Proud of them both, we are. Proud of the two of them."

"*The two of them*," echoed Rhidian, wistfully. To the boy, the expression had an unfortunate ring to it. After all, there was still the unfinished business over whether Valeria would accept Rhidian's hand in marriage.

"Surely you are not dispirited, Rhidian?" inquired Aaron. "Is this not the day when your tribe was freed from bondage and when the sacred manuscripts – the Lord be praised – were finally saved from destruction?"

"Just so," agreed Eifiona. "Why, we have even received a promise, this very hour, that a large consignment of scrolls, previously earmarked for destruction, are now to be forwarded to us instead. And who do you think it was who sent us that promise? Caesar of these islands, Constantius Chlorus, no less!"

"Constantius?" inquired Valeria, looking puzzled. "He's miles away on the other side of the country. How could you have heard from him?"

Eifiona tapped her nose, mysteriously. "I believe there was a pigeon involved, somewhere along the line; except that, because the bird didn't know its way here, the message had to be relayed to us by an envoy on horseback. The envoy is still here, in fact. He was sent on the errand by your father, Valeria."

"My father?" queried the girl. "Where is he now?"

"Not too far away, it seems. He is anxious to see you, of course. Is there any message you wish to send him? I am sure the envoy would be happy to take it."

Valeria was silent for a moment, a frown etched on her face. Then, suddenly, her expression broke into a grin.

"I do indeed have a message," she announced. "Perhaps the envoy could ask my father to proceed directly here, to the place where the waters meet, where I propose to hold a ceremony – a ceremony to announce my betrothal."

A gasp of surprise went up from among those standing nearby. Aaron was the first to comment.

"Child," said the pedlar, softly, "you have not yet told us who is to be the object of your affections."

Valeria smiled. "I think you know him. He's a local boy."

With that, the girl flung her arms around Rhidian and snuggled up against his chest in a display of unmistakable exuberance. It was a performance that the bashful Rhidian at first found difficult to match, mindful as he was of the inquisitive band of witnesses gathered all around. Nevertheless, nothing could repress the boy for long. He was soon cradling Valeria in his arms with the gallantry of a veteran.

It turned out to be the signal that all the onlookers were waiting for – they began to cheer. Indeed, so heartfelt was the sense of occasion, in the wake of the earlier battle victory, that a great roar of rejoicing swept through the whole gathering, accompanied by cries of "Praise the Lord". Nor did the celebrations end there.

Before long, fires were being kindled and a feast prepared, something that the Gwenfo folk were able to put together from their reserves of food inside the Dinas. A quantity of elderflower wine, of mysterious vintage, was also made available which, no doubt, contributed to the eccentricity of the dancing that was soon underway.

When the revelry finally began to abate, Rhidian and Valeria withdrew from the gathering and, at length, found themselves wandering alone along the banks of the *Woad*. As they did so, they became aware that the character and appearance of the pool had changed once more. It had reverted to its former state. The ochre tinge had waned, the swollen waters had subsided, and the raging currents of the vortex had been stilled, restoring the motions of the pool to a benign cycle of gently-lapping waves; but for how long?

If a passer-by had stood where Rhidian and Valeria had stood on that day, he would have observed, beside the *Woad*, the rock with the painting of Jesus upon it. What might he have made of it? Would he have been able to guess whom it represented? Would it have lingered in his imagination as he went upon his way, causing him to desire nothing less than to know the truth about the person in the picture? And what then for the thinker of such thoughts? Would he have chosen to remain a passer-by, or have become worthy of a different name?